Christmas at Crazy Woman Creek

Ryan Jo *Summers*

CHRISTMAS AT CRAZY WOMAN CREEK

ISBN: 979-8-88653-181-7

Published by Satin Romance
An Imprint of Melange Books, LLC
White Bear Lake, MN 55110
www.satinromance.com

Published in the United States of America.

Cover Design by Caroline Andrus

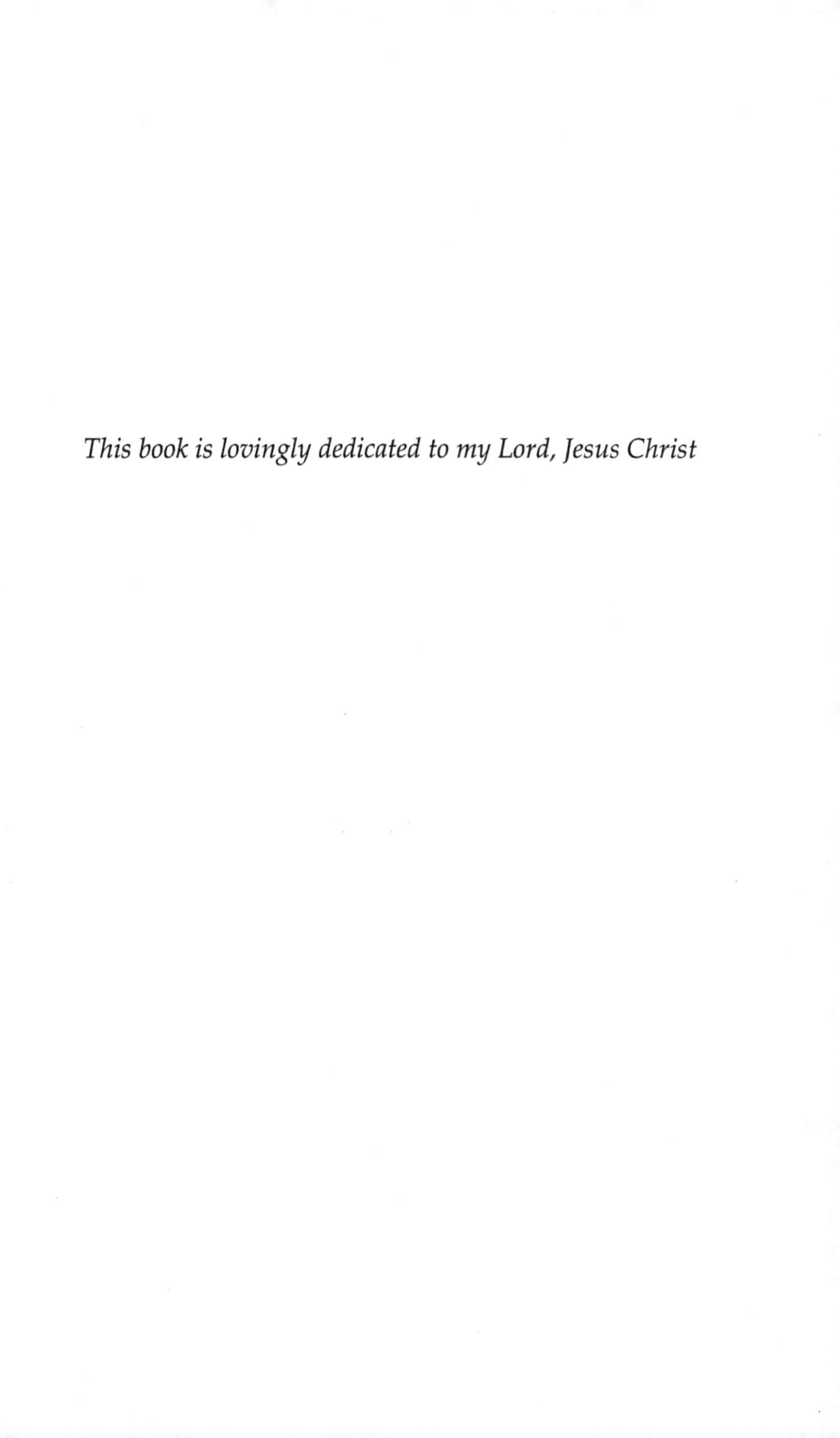

This book is lovingly dedicated to my Lord, Jesus Christ

THE LEGEND OF CRAZY WOMAN CREEK

Back in days when horses ran wild and Native Americans shared the land, a great river stretched between two tribes: the Comanche and the Kiowa.

On one side lived Bear Paw, a promising young warrior. He stood tall and straight among his people. On the other side was Red Feathers, the prettiest maiden in all the land. Each brave wanted Red Feathers, but Bear Paw loved her the most. He brought ponies and furs to her father and the two young lovers planned to marry.

Then a great war broke out among many different tribes. Bear Paw kissed Red Feathers and promised to return soon. Then they would marry and have a big celebration. But an arrow pierced his heart, and he died in battle. Word came back to Red Feathers.

She rode her pony into the great river, wailing her song of mourning. She lifted her arms high to the skies, her screams of grief echoing off the rock walls and towering trees. Her true love was gone, and her heart bled long and deep.

Both tribes could hear her screams and cries all that day, and all that night, and through the following day. She was senseless in her grief. Crazy, as some called her. Then, in the darkness of the second day, her mourning silenced. Her pony returned alone. They went to search for Red Feathers, but she was never seen again. The river turned blood red in color.

To this very day, on still nights and foggy mornings, when you go near the water, you can hear the anguished cries of a woman—crazy with grief. Sometimes folks will see her moccasin footprints along the shore, leading into the water. And sometimes, depending on the moon and time of year, the water runs blood red.

CHAPTER
ONE

The place would give a strong man the chills, even on the brightest day. Stretching out from the dark foothills above and winding along the valley thick with pines and scrub trees, the towering rock and rushing waters had a way of mocking a person. Of making them feel insignificant. Brave travelers swore they heard the scream of a woman, especially on full moon winter nights. Maybe there was something to the old legend: a grief-stricken woman and her endless cries of crazy, sad pain. Though he'd never seen the river run red, this sure felt like the place that could happen. It wouldn't have surprised him.

Colby Lonigan shivered and yanked his denim jacket tighter, drawing the collar up. Trust these stupid cows to wander into this god-forsaken place. The wind picked up, howling with a dreadful wail, setting Colby's teeth on edge. Sensing his unease, his buckskin gelding beneath him flattened his ears, snorted, and shied.

"Easy, boy." He tightened the reins. "Just the wind." He patted Ben's neck reassuringly. How had such a nice day turned into a dark, cool, windy hour simply by riding into the dismal Crazy Woman creek area? Life's mysteries, he supposed. Or the legend.

He didn't necessarily believe the old legend, not like some folks did. But he'd never come to the Crazy Woman creek area that it wasn't cold, dark, and plain eerie. Even now, the rest of his ranch was blanketed in mid-December snow, glistening with pre-Christmas light. Life held a festive air. Once he topped the ridge and started down into the Crazy Woman range, the air was noticeably colder. Here, it was hard to imagine Christmas was just around the corner. Colby snickered. Here, he'd believe Armageddon was a lot closer than Christmas.

Ben's hooves clattered along the loose gravel, and he skirted scrubby trees and brush. Bawling reached his ears and he almost whooped for joy. Gratefully, he reined Ben toward the scrub trees the sound came from. "C'mon, Ben, let's go round up those fool critters." Personally, he couldn't get out of there fast enough.

He could just make out the white, black, brown, and brindle patterns of the cows hidden among the branches when Ben snorted and shied again. Nearly unseated, Colby tapped his heels against the horse's flanks.

"Ben! What the hell?"

A new sound, a low moan surfaced, distinguishing itself from the bawling of the cows. He followed Ben's nervous eye rolls to a low bush, full of thick evergreen boughs.

He squinted and made out…cloth, not cowhide. Cold shivers raced over him at the sight of a shoeless, slender foot.

"It's a human!" Jumping from the saddle, Colby removed his .45 Colt handgun from the holster at his belt—

just in case—and cautiously approached the prone figure on the ground.

Colby dropped to one knee and parted the branches. His eyes widened and his breath hitched at the sight of the unresponsive woman dressed in ivory slacks and a peach ruffled blouse. Bruises and red scratches marred her face and arms. Twigs and leaves tangled in her long, dark hair. His pulse raced and he scrubbed his jaw, thinking fast. Then he swallowed hard and tapped her shoulder.

"Ma'am? Can you hear me? Are you alright?" He never understood why one was supposed to ask that last question when the answer seemed obvious. *Hell no, she wasn't all right, you dummy.* "Ma'am?" He gave her another—less gentle—shake.

Moaning softly, her eyelids fluttered open. She blinked rapidly and finally settled on him. He smiled at her confused, coffee-brown eyes.

"Howdy." He tipped his hat. "My name's Colby Lonigan." When she failed to respond, he jerked his thumb over his shoulder. "That's Ben, my horse." She gave a nod, stopping as if it hurt. Fresh spikes of fear raced over Colby. "Ma'am, is anything broken? Can you get up?" He looked around. "And where is your horse?" *Poorly trained critter to take off after losing its rider.* Ben would stay with him until he was ordered to return home.

He holstered his .45 handgun and searched around for her missing shoe. This was going to be tricky. He rocked back on his heels and pushed his hat back. "Can you tell me how you ended up way out here alone?"

She slowly scooted to a sitting position, and he could tell it hurt. She grit her teeth and the spark in her eye told him she had a fire in her soul. Instantly, he found himself drawn to her spirit, her sand, and her grit. All great qualities he admired. Then he noticed the dried trail of blood behind her right ear.

"Where is this?" she asked, her voice just above a faint whisper.

Startled, Colby stared for a moment. "Are you saying you're lost? This is Crazy Woman Creek." He gestured toward the sound of the river flowing nearby. "I'm hunting my cattle over yonder. Hear 'em bawling? My ranch, The Tica, is just over that ridge there. It butts up to the Crazy Woman Creek. I raise Herefords and Longhorns."

She followed his hands blankly as he directed and pointed. Finally she drew her knees to her chest and wrapped her arms around her knees as if she was cold. Immediately, he shrugged off his lined denim jacket and draped it around her slender shoulders, not helping but to inhale her perfume. Flowers and fruit. He liked it.

"That better, Ma'am?" At her stiff nod, he settled back on his heels again, studying her. What a predicament. "So what can you tell me about how you came to be out here?"

She looked out across the landscape, drew her lower lip in, and gave him a sad shake of her head. "I don't know."

What did she mean? Thunderbolts of worry shot through him in cold slices. "Was anyone else with you?"

This time tears formed in her eyes, and she blinked them away. "I don't know."

Colby's heart thumped fast, like when Sierra told him she had something to tell him, and she knew he wasn't going to like it. That same dark feeling of foreboding. Dread. *Oh shit.* He wet his lips. The cattle bawled. A coyote howled. "Ma'am. Will you please tell me your name?"

She huddled closer into his jacket, shivering a little, and

cast an anxious look around. Fresh tears misted on her dark eyelashes. "I would if I knew it myself."

Her words softened as a whisper in the wind, punched Colby in the gut, leaving him weak. Damnation! *Amnesia!* That sure explained a lot. But how the devil did a lone woman get way out here, afoot, missing her shoe, and injured? It was probable her mount spooked at something, threw her, and took off. Except, where did she come from? She wasn't a local and she sure wasn't dressed for a ride in the mountains.

Better yet, now that he'd found her, what was he going to do about her? As Sierra was fond of saying, Finders Keepers. That hardly applied in this case, but it was a starting point. Swallowing his many misgivings, he pasted on a smile that he hoped looked friendly and reassuring, because he reckoned she sure needed friendly and reassuring about now. His rogue cattle would just have to wait. He pulled in an unsteady breath.

"There's dirt and blood under your fingernails, ma'am. Do you know how that came to be?"

He watched her gaze down at her extended hands, then back at him with unspoken questions in her eyes. The sad shake of her head made his stomach roll. Well, he couldn't just leave her out here by herself. There seemed only one solution for the moment.

"Ma'am, like I said, my name's Colby. Do you reckon you can sit up there on top of Ben with me?"

Her bewildered gaze traveled to the grazing horse before returning to him. Long enough for him to think of a plan.

"To where?"

"My ranch, The Tica." He nodded northeasterly. "You can clean up, rest, and get a bit of grub." He shrugged. *And hopefully, remember who you are.* "Decide if there is anyone we can call to come and get you."

She seemed to consider his offer, as if she had others to compare it against. He smiled, amused at her fortitude even now. Most folks would have jumped at the offer of a rescue with both hands waving. Little Miss Tough-As-Nails would take his rescue—probably—but she'd also make sure he knew she would not be beholding to him. Oh yeah, he liked her a lot.

"All right. Fine."

Yep, he sure liked her plenty. Likely too much. Especially for a lady who didn't even know who she was.

CHAPTER
TWO

She gazed at the big, light brown horse as it cropped dried grass poking through the snow by the trees. A shiver involuntarily stole over her, despite the warmth and hay smell of the jacket. She returned her attention to the man and his question. Rugged. In a word, that would be how she would describe Colby. Ruggedly built. He appeared as solidly built as the trees around them. Ruggedly handsome. Her fingers yearned to tug at his thick dark hair poking out through his hat and play with his equally dark beard. Ruggedly commanding. He took charge while she failed to produce something as simple as her own name or how she came to be out here in this desolate wilderness. Both were absolute mysteries to her. All she knew for sure was she was cold and hurt all over and scared.

His piercing blue eyes studied her with intelligence and patience, and a touch of amusement. She wondered what he found so amusing while pain racked her head and jarred most of her body and frustration gnawed at her. One thing she felt certain of, however, was that she had never been on a horse.

"Ready, Ma'am?"

No, but she lacked better offers or suggestions. She sucked in a painful breath and gripped his hand. She felt the gentle strength that promised a greater strength, and the hardened callouses. Electricity passed between them like tiny slivers of lightning. Had he felt them too, or was she delusional as well? She met his crystal blue eyes again, feeling her heartbeat skip a few paces and her mouth move into an 'O' of bewildered surprise.

"Ma'am?"

She shook her head, regretting the motion as fresh pain raced through her brain, followed by warm blood trickling from the wound by her temple.

"Wait a second. Here." Colby must have noticed it, too. He propped her against a tree trunk and unknotted the red handkerchief tied around his throat. He folded it into squares and gently pushed her hair aside. He laid the folded cloth over the wound and guided her finger to it. "Hold that steady till it sets. I'll fix it proper once we get to the ranch."

The cloth felt warm against her skin, and she breathed in his musky, woodsy scent. She was beginning to look forward to the ranch place he called Tica for several reasons.

He studied her, eyes anxiously darting over her. Now, just inches separating them, she smelled the cinnamon on his breath. Gum?

"Lean on me. We'll still be an awkward hobble, but we can't have you strutting around without two shoes."

She wordlessly complied, wrapping her arm around his torso. Beneath his rough flannel shirt, she felt his tight, corded muscles and washboard abs. She instinctively knew she'd felt slender men before, but none as fit and well-developed as Colby. How could she be so sure of that and not know her own name?

Gravel crunched under his boots as he guided and carried her to the horse. It looked bigger now that she stood beside it. She felt the heat coming off its body and it turned to look at her, with large brown eyes and stringy grass hanging out of its mouth. Before she could protest or think this through, Colby gingerly lifted her up into the saddle as though she were made of porcelain.

"Are you sure he can carry both of us?" she asked as he swung up in front of her.

She felt his laughter as she curled her arms around his middle. "Doubt he'll notice the difference." He clicked his tongue once. "Get up, boy."

She felt him lean to the left and the horse turned left. As it lurched, she slid into Colby and tightened her grip. "Oh!" The startled exclamation spilled out as she vainly swung her feet in a pitiful attempt to find something to hold onto.

"Hold tight to me. We'll be to Tica in no time."

The horse had a rhythmic step once he found it as he plowed through the dried grass and she rested her cheek against the coarse cotton of Colby's shoulder, closing her eyes. Muscles slid beneath the fabric as he controlled the horse, but she barely noticed. All she knew was the cinnamon scent wafting back and the soft words he spoke to the horse.

"Where did you say we were?"

"Crazy Woman Range. Town's called Crazy Woman too. Henderson County, Texas."

Texas? What was she doing in Texas? Intuitively, she knew this was not home. Vacation? Business trip? So where was home? Who was she traveling with? Or was she traveling alone? Thinking about it only made her head pound more. She focused on the rumble of his voice.

She was almost asleep when she felt the shift in the horse's stride. "Good boy," Colby praised. She pried her heavy eyelids open and looked around. Brown fencing stretched for miles. Horses milled along some fencing and cows dotted others. White clouds spread all the way to the distant hills and trees. Flanked by tall, red barns stood a two-story stone house wrapped in a long porch and multiple balconies. A huge bronze star graced the bricks of the chimney rising to greet the blue sky.

"Yours?"

"Yep. Tica." She smiled at the pride in his voice. Even in the dead of winter, the house and buildings appeared well-maintained, and the animals seemed happy.

Two snowmen stood guard outside the house, one short with a two-ball body and the other one taller with three snowballs forming the body. Both wore button smiles and carrot noses. She had to smile at the lopsided creations. She noticed the snow hadn't been as deep once they started over the top of the hills and the air was warmer. Whatever snow had been on the ground was now used to create the snowmen guards.

He brought the horse to a stop in front of the house and held out his arm and she grabbed hold to swing down. Within seconds, he joined her, searching her face. His brows puckered in concern. "Lean on me. You look pale."

Exhausted, she nodded. What was his wife going to think of him bringing an unknown woman inside? They slowly made their way along the sidewalk, up the three steps to the porch and along the wood plank flooring.

They entered through a side door. Stunned, she realized the door wasn't even locked. Somewhere in the recess of her mind she pictured an elaborate home security system with a keypad and robotic voice. Was it hers? If so, what did the actual house look like? Nothing solid came to mind.

"We're as awkward as a three-legged sack race, but we'll get there," Colby said, cutting her a grin as they crossed the threshold. "I could carry you."

Her throbbing foot cried out in favor of that and images of his strong arms hefting her like some sort of prize filled her mind. Sudden heat rushed over her, blood pumped, and she feared her wound might spring another leak. "Umm, no, this is fine. You did say we're almost there?" Was it just her or did she sound disappointed? If he noticed, he gave no indication.

For distraction, she studied her surroundings. Vaulted ceilings with wood beams, large, ample windows flooded with winter daylight and overstuffed contemporary furniture in neutral colors. A few green plants spread their stalks toward the light. Photos of a blonde-haired, blue-eyed girl decorated the walls either in school poses or playing outside in some barnyard scene. Some had her riding a pony, wearing a big smile, long braid down her back, and a huge hat on her head. The two people completely absent from any pictures were the little girl's parents. Colby and his wife?

The Christmas tree stood in the corner of the living room, beside the huge stone fireplace soaring toward the wood-beamed ceiling. White lights lit up the corner, shining on cardboard boxes taped and stacked around it. She spelled out the words 'decorations' scribbled in black marker on each of them.

"We got the tree up a couple of days ago," Colby said,

following her gaze. "Still need to find the time to get all the decorations and gaiety out and up."

She pondered that. "I'm sorry to take you away from your obligations."

"No need to apologize, Ma'am. The herd will get rounded up; the decorations will get put up. Right now, my concern is you."

He turned to gaze at her, and she searched his face, looking for… She had no clue what she was looking for. His sincere worry took her by surprise, and she had no idea why. Mutely, she nodded. What could she say?

"Here it is, the downstairs guest suite." Colby reached past her and swung open the door. "Queen bed, soaker tub, television, and a private patio." He swallowed as he turned back to her. "A bath will give you a chance to wash that dirt and dried blood off. You might never want to leave." He chuckled, then sobered. "Umm. I'll go see about your meal. Ma'am." Tipping his hat brim, he spun around.

By the time she had finished a refreshingly warm soak and redressed, she felt better. Though still torn, her fingernails were cleaner, and her foot throbbed less. She sat on the bed, staring at the image of the unknown woman staring back at her from the mirror mounted over the dresser several feet away. A knock startled her. "Yes?"

Colby entered, balancing a tray. Steaming aromas escaped to tease her stomach.

"I wasn't sure what you like, so I stuck with basic soup, a salad, garlic bread, and herbal tea. How's that sound?" He set the large tray on the dresser.

"It sounds very good. Thank you." Since her mouth was watering, it told her either that was her favorite dish or most likely, she hadn't eaten in a while. Her pinched stomach rumbled in eager anticipation as she debated where to begin.

"I could bring a chair and small table in if you'd like."

She shook her head. "That's not necessary. I can eat sitting there." She motioned to the bed. He already did so much for her, she'd hate to ask him to bring extra furniture in too.

"I wish I had some other clothes for you. And shoes." He shifted the tray over to the bed and leaned back against the wall beside the dresser.

She smiled at Colby's comment and wiggled her bare toes on the cool slate stones, looking at the bright red nail polish. The manicured appearance and soft skin suggested she wore shoes and cared for her feet. So who was she? Swallowing a sigh, she picked up the buttery garlic bread, not able to ignore the rich aroma any longer. "You weren't expecting guests with no luggage to show up. The bath and this are plenty, really."

He grinned. "Don't get too quick with the praise. The soup is from canned concentrate, the bread was frozen, and the salad came from a pre-mixed bag." He lifted his shoulder in a shrug. "I'm not much of a short notice cook, but I try."

She took a few more bites of bread, strong with garlic, savoring it on her tongue. The tomato sauce, yeast, garlic, and herbs all spelled comfort to her soul. She didn't remember a meal like this, but she knew in her heart it was familiar and good. "Frozen or not, it's still fine." She licked her lips and sipped the tea. She might as well ask the question she wondered the most. "Your, umm, wife, is all right with my presence?"

His lips thinned and he folded his arms, his body going rigid. "There is no wife, though you doubtlessly will meet my daughter soon. Sierra, she's seven."

"I'm sorry. Did something—"

He held his palm out. "No, there's no tragic tale to tell. She's gone of her own accord. I have Sierra and Tica. That's plenty for me. It's you, Ma'am, I wonder about." His tone softened. He stepped to her side and touched her wrist. His calloused fingertip moved up and traced a pale circle around her left ring finger. Stunned, she stared at it, the implication slowly sinking in.

Married? Was she married? Engaged? That was what he was insinuating. If so, where was her husband or betrothed? Was she divorced? Widowed? The warm bread turned to paste in her mouth. She lifted her eyes to see the same questions mirrored back in Colby's eyes and she swallowed the hard lump. Horror filled her throat as she lowered her gaze to her still-dirty fingernails, suddenly feeling as stained as her fingers.

"I don't know," she admitted in a hoarse whisper. She peeked up toward him.

He looked like she'd just slapped him. Well, she felt like she'd just been slapped. What if her husband was still out there, lost in the wilderness somewhere? Injured or dead?

Colby patted her shoulder. "That's okay, it'll come. In the meantime, I've got to call you something besides ma'am. How do you feel about the name Faith?"

Faith. She tried the name on, mentally saying it to herself. It wasn't familiar, but it felt comfortable. It would work. "I like it. Anyone particular?"

"No, just a name I've always liked. I wanted it to be Sierra's middle name, but somehow it got switched after I left the hospital. I've never had another chance to name anyone, so now seems like a good time."

She glanced down at her fingers, the pale ring around one, the scratches and cuts and the chipped nails. She studied the evidence that not long ago they had been trimmed and painted a pretty shade of rosy red. She had no callouses on her fingertips. What did she do? What happened to her? If her hands could only talk…

She sighed and met Colby's patient gaze. "Yes, that is fine. Faith it is."

CHAPTER THREE

Colby returned home; three plastic bags looped through his fingers. Giggles floated from down the hall as he entered, and he smiled. Maybe Sierra could help Faith regain her memories. Another thought followed that one. If she were married, could she have children? What if some baby or small child was out there, somewhere, wondering where its mama was? His chest ached at the idea.

"Sierra?" he called down the hall.

A delighted squeal responded, and he followed the sound to Faith's room. Sierra met him at the doorway, crushing him into a little girl's bear hug. He tugged affectionately at her long blonde braid, inhaling the strawberry peach scent of her shampoo, unable to stop the smile on his face each time he got her bearhugs.

"Have a good day, Button?"

"Yes!"

She launched into a monologue describing who did what

at school while skillfully dodging his playful tries to tug her braid again. While his mind listened to his daughter's happy chatter, his gaze sought Faith.

She sat on the edge of the bed; her hands folded neatly on her lap as she watched their exchange. He'd be willing to bet Sierra had been seated next to her and doubtlessly regaling Ms. Faith with exciting tales of the day. What had she initially thought of his social butterfly daughter? Now her expression was a mix of curiosity and amusement. Papers—homework?—stacked beside her drew him across the room, Sierra chattered away, pressing near his side.

"I brought you some things," he said when Sierra stopped to catch a breath. He held the plastic shopping bags out to Faith.

She arched one dark eyebrow and reached for them. She glanced in them and then faced him; her brows puckered in surprise. "I hadn't realized you'd gone to town."

"Naw, I just ran down to The Plaza. It's not part of Crazy Woman, it's just a collection of buildings strung together. Dollar store, car wash, thrift store, and a few other little things."

"Uncle Jack says The Plaza is like lights on a Christmas tree," Sierra chimed in. "Some good bulbs and some duds."

"Uncle Jack?"

"My foreman. And my best friend since first grade. And surrogate second daddy to Sierra too, I reckon."

Faith gave a slow nod. He set the last bag down next to the others and scooped up Sierra's papers. "We'll leave you to this and go finish Button's schoolwork."

❄

Half an hour later, Sierra closed her book and set about preparing the table for dinner. Colby watched, grinning as she added an extra plate and table service to the normal three spots they used. He decided not to mention anything and returned to the makings for a hearty son-of-a-gun stew casserole. He hadn't lied to Faith. He could cook okay; it was just that his cooking skills were limited. Eggs, stews, grilled meats and macaroni and cheese were his specialties. Neither Sierra nor Jack ever complained.

"Daddy, can I go outside now?"

He studied the table. It all looked good. "Sure thing, Button. Be back in thirty."

With a promise, she was gone like a shot from a rifle. He crossed to the Dutch door that opened to the screened-in porch and swung the bottom half closed, leaving the top half still open. This would give him better access to hear any shouts. And it helped cool the room, which was more beneficial in the summer. Either way, he liked having an ear able to hear Sierra. It was worth the cool air entering the room to be able to know she was safe.

He devoted his thoughts to stirring the beef and draining the pasta. He could multitask! He dumped a couple of cans of tomatoes and beans into the pasta and added a generous helping of chili powder, chopped garlic, onions, and minced green pepper. He and Sierra could never have enough flavor in their foods.

The sporadic cow bawl wafted in. The mournful cry and cool wind reminded him of the Crazy Woman Creek, which took his thoughts immediately over to Faith.

She'd seemed genuinely surprised at the purchases he'd brought. It was just some clothing from the thrift store and a few toiletries from the dollar store. The toothbrush and toothpaste seemed like no brainers to him. He'd tossed in a red hairbrush and barrette to match her red nail polish as he couldn't imagine Sierra's pink Barbie brush working through her thick dark tangles. He sighed and stirred. Even disheveled as she was, Faith was a lovely woman.

What was Faith doing? Did she like the clothes? Did he—?

"Is your door broken?"

He jumped at her soft question. His head jerked up from his work on the stove and he realized he had not heard her because she was stocking footed. She wore green plaid knickers and a blood red top with ruffles along the neckline. Hell's bells. Had he really picked that out? Mercy! She looked like someone's granny fixing to go golf-ing. He'd always thought golf courses were a waste of a good piece of land. And now he decided her ugly clothing was a waste of yardage of clothing on a beautiful woman. One of his old T-shirts would be better. What had he been thinking? Was everything he got her as hideous as this outfit?

He'd just grabbed some things off the thrift store racks that looked like they might fit her. He'd failed to picture her true size and seriously underestimated her shape and form. Well, he'd just proven the fact that men can't shop. And she looked terrible. He could smack himself.

He hastily ladled the beef into the pasta and tomato/ bean mixture and heaved the wooden spoon through it as embarrassment fanned his cheeks. Hopefully she'd think it was just heat from the stove.

At least she was game about it, and not complaining. Then he realized she was looking over his shoulder at the door. Had her question been serious?

"Naw, it's not broken. It's supposed to be split like that. It's called a Dutch door. Haven't you ever seen a Dutch?"

"Do I look Dutch to you?"

From the look in her eyes, he had a feeling she was talking about more than a door. Her silent agony slammed into him. What was it like to know absolutely nothing about yourself? He shoved the casserole into the warmed oven and reached for her hands. He rubbed his thumbs over the smooth skin of her wrists, studying her dark eyes. The color reminded him of a rich cup of coffee. "Naw. If I had to guess, I'd say…. probably Italian."

He guided her to the mirror in the parlor and sat her down facing it. Gently, he traced her face, locking his gaze with her large, dark, and luminous eyes in the mirror. Her hair smelled fruity and clean, and the tropical scent wafted around him. Mango and pineapple. His pulse skipped and he swallowed a hard lump.

"You have a heart-shaped face, red rose bud lips, and your complexion is olive. Your cheekbones are high." Slowly, he outlined each part with his fingertips as he spoke, carefully moving along her face and neck, down to her delicate collarbone. She watched each move, her eyes fixed on him in the mirror. When he first saw her down at the Crazy Woman, he thought she was a pretty lady. Now, he saw her true beauty and it stalled him.

"And I noticed the first food you went for was the most Italian-smelling one. It came from frozen, but it still had the tomatoes, cheeses, and spices of Italian garlic bread and you seemed to really enjoy it."

She swallowed; her throat moving, though her gaze remained locked on his. "Have you known many Italian women?"

"You're my first."

Colby turned her around gently by her shoulders, cupped his fingers under her chin and tipped her face up. Leaning down, he kissed her, feeling her warm skin. Tropical scents from her bath rose where his fingers brushed, and he tasted the fresh mint of her toothpaste. She was soft in his arms, and he could tell she was unsure how to react to him.

Easing her up, he brought her close, deepening the kiss. She slowly yielded to him, growing bolder as he held his patience. He liked it that she had to think about what she wanted to do. Fresh desire swept over him, and a low groan built from his throat and escaped his lips. His fingers gripped the worn fabric of her granny's shirt and he yearned to yank it off her but sensed that would be too much for her. There were too many unanswered questions at the moment. However, he was a patient man, and he knew she felt the sparks zapping between them as much as he did. He heard the low moan rumbling from her throat and saw how she closed her eyes and relaxed her face as yearning pulsed through her.

Then the buzz of the oven timer startled them both. Colby pulled back, taking pleasure in Faith's reddened cheeks and lips roughened by his beard. She licked them, and he hoped she tasted him. He hauled in a ragged breath, and slowly stroked a knuckle down her face, winking. He inclined his head toward the dining room.

"Go ahead, take a seat in there. I'll go ring the dinner bell for Sierra and Jack."

Faith wobbled over to the table, her senses reeling. The hairs along her arms and back of her neck still stood up. Was she the only one who'd heard music playing? Or felt electricity crackling through the air? She sat, and gazed out the window at the dirt driveway, dirt road, and trees beyond, as her pulse raced like cars on the freeway.

She was a long way from a freeway here. She traced the outline of a ring pattern on her left finger. Even if she had a husband, she just knew he had never made her feel so alive, so special as Colby had in the last few moments. Was he really her husband or lover if she could not remember him?

Sierra arrived, giggling at something a rail thin man said. He was dressed like Colby in a plaid button shirt and blue jeans. Seeing him did not set her pulse racing like watching Colby did. Catching her eye, he removed his hat and stuck out his hand.

"Jack Jennings, Ma'am. You must be that stray heifer that Colby found down by the Crazy Woman."

Faith blinked, taken aback. She shook his rough-skinned hand before agreeing, "I suppose so. I'm Faith."

"Daddy's calling her that 'cause she don't remember her own name," Sierra supplied brightly.

Faith appreciated her innocence, even if her grammar needed work, but felt her cheeks grow warm nonetheless under Jack's sympathetic stare. Thankfully, he took his chair, two down from her.

"Must be hard, Ma'am. The Lord knows there's things I'd like to un-remember, like a marriage or two, but there's a whole lot I'd sure hate to forget. My condolences."

"Thank you. Colby seems to think it's only temporary."

Jack grinned. "Ma'am, Colby would look at a spinning

tornado and say: "Aw, shucks, it's only temporary.". He sees the silver lining in every cloud, or he paints one there himself."

Faith smiled, unable to help but like the lanky cowboy. His slow drawl was similar to Colby's, and a sharp contrast from Sierra's energetic chirp. Sierra reminded Faith of a bird. Colby's lolling accent carried a sexy tone that excited her. Jack just made her smile at his wit.

"Dinner is served," Colby announced as he entered the room and set a large glass dish in the center of the table. Smells escaped, lifting into the air, and Faith tried to identify them. She singled out the beefy and nutty scents, and the rich tomatoes sung to her soul. So what did that mean?

"Son-of-a-gun stew, turned into a casserole. Male cooking specialty," Colby explained, sitting down, and reaching for Sierra and Jack's hands. Sierra and Jack each reached for one of Faith's hands and together, they formed a perfect square.

Astonished, Faith watched as they all bowed their heads and Colby prayed. He ended a few sentences later with a thankful comment for her safe rescue and a swift recovery of her memories. Sierra snuck a peek over at her.

"Don't you pray before meals?" the girl asked after everyone released their hands and began passing plates.

Evidently not. She glanced at Colby as he heaped food on a plate and passed it on. Wherever she was from, meals were never handled like this. "Guess I simply forgot."

Dinner was a good—albeit unusual—event. Faith knew she'd never tasted a meal like Colby's all-in-one casserole or shared such animated, colorful conversation like she did with Sierra and Jack. Together, they were hysterical. She particularly enjoyed the childhood stories told at Colby's expense and to Sierra's acute interest. Her heart tugged at the loving way he interacted with Sierra and the brotherly way he was with Jack. It was a tight, devoted triangle she was suddenly in the middle of and the emotions and pleasures it created in her were undoubtedly something new. She knew this, amnesia or not.

So what had she left behind her?

"I'll do the dishes," she volunteered as dinner and conversation wound down. Jack had said earlier he and Colby enjoyed going out on the porch after dinner to talk shop. She was eager to repay him for his kindness, and washing their dishes was a good start.

Colby kicked the toe of his boot against the porch railing, setting the rocking chair back and forth as he watched the sun slowly sinking over the snow-covered mountaintop. Normally, this sight stirred feelings of peacefulness and relaxation within his soul. Not tonight. Tonight, he was keyed up and not feeling much inner peace.

Behind him, he heard the clank of dishes. Jack hadn't hung around too long. That was fine by him. He wasn't feeling particularly neighborly. Right now, he had two big headaches on his mind and appreciated a bit of time alone. He took a pull on the beer in his hand and then set the cold bottle on the porch floor. The cool temperature of the beer matched the brisk wind around him and he hunkered deeper into his denim jacket.

Next, he withdrew the envelope curled in his pocket and fingered the broken seal. His lip curled into a snarl at the legal notice informing him his former in-laws were suing him for custody of Sierra. Like hell. He'd fight till he was out of breath and dead in the ground before they got his daughter. Not his Button.

And Faith. Eagle-eyed Jack pointed out how some of the bruises along her arms were older and already fading to green. Others were fresh, but not as new as the one- and two-day ones. He'd simply assumed they had all been caused by a spill off a horse, but Jack felt certain they had nothing to do with falling off her missing horse. So who the hell had been laying bruises on her? Did it have anything to do with that pale circle around her ring finger and why there was no ring there now?

Plus, when Jack rode back to the Creek to collect the stray herd, he reported he'd only found one set of horse tracks… Ben's. But he'd tracked Faith's footprints and she'd been on foot for well over a mile, and minus one shoe.

And what was worse—this all really bothered him. He was liking Faith far more than he should for a lady he just rescued. To see fresh wounds on her body was bad enough but alongside older bruises made him mad enough to go punch a bull in the eye. His protective instincts were flaring off like rockets between Sierra and his former in-laws and now Faith and her troubles. Lord, what was he supposed to do?

He reached down for the beer and took another swallow. The sun dipped below the mountain, blanketing the ranch in darkness. The dusk-to-dawn lights kicked on, illuminating the swept and cleared paths from house to barns to bunkhouse. He no longer heard the clatter of dishes.

The mooing of cows settling for the evening and the occasional snort of a horse accented the cold dark. Somewhere a night bird called. For the moment, Colby envied the nightlife and their peace and simplicity.

CHAPTER **FOUR**

Faith jerked awake, gasping for breath. What dreadful noise woke her? Scooting up, she hugged the pillow to her chest, cringing as the sound rolled across the yard again. The terror-filled scream of a woman being killed.

Where was Colby? Or Jack? She swallowed. Where was Sierra? Fear for the child goaded her out of bed. One more screech set her teeth on edge. Who was being murdered out there? She slipped from her room and padded barefoot across the cold tile floor to the kitchen. Daylight shone dimly through the uncovered windows, but the room was still shrouded in darkness. Nightlights gave enough glow for her to spot a black skillet setting on the stove.

She gripped it, scooped it up, and almost dropped it. It was much heavier than it looked. Adjusting her grip, she headed for the door as another ear-splitting wail of terror sent shivers racing down her spine. Where the heck were the men?

Carefully, teeth set, nerves tight, and breath held, she twisted the knob and eased the door open enough to slide out. The yard lights flickered off as daylight spilled over the white-capped mountains. It was a breathtaking view, but she took no opportunity to enjoy it now. She glanced around, heart hammering. Her breath came in frosty puffs. Horses snorted and cows mooed. Another shriek made her jump.

"Morning, Faith."

Gasping, she whirled and dropped the pan. It landed with a heavy thud on the wood planks. Her hands went to her chest. Colby sat in the rocker; feet propped on the railing. Despite the on-going murder and wails, she took the time to appreciate the beautiful picture he made just sitting there. Yummy.

"What are you doing?" she finally asked once her breath and wits recovered. How was he so calm while those wails and shrieks rent the air?

"Thinking mostly."

"What about that?" She flung her arm out toward the region of the shrieks.

He lifted a dark eyebrow, and she caught a whiff of cinnamon gum again. She took a step closer. "The screams?" She clarified.

"You mean Buster?" He chuckled. "He does have a horrible sounding crow, I admit, but he is the most dependable rooster I've ever known. Sounds like a gang of stray cats caterwauling each morning, but he loves it when Sierra reads her schoolbooks to him. Fool bird is almost her pet."

She stood, her jaw drooping, trying to make sense of his words. His slow drawl assured her there was no danger. So a rooster was a— Fool bird—

"What were you planning to do with the cast iron?"

She followed his gaze down to the pan at her feet.

Embarrassment flooded her face as she failed to find words to describe her misunderstanding. She wriggled her bare toes in awkward silence. Finally, she noticed the cold. Colby stood up, stepped close, and cupped his hands around her face. His smile was tender.

"I appreciate your bravery, Faith. That speaks volumes about your character. A cast iron pan is a great weapon to take into a fight too. Remember that." He released her and stepped back. "That old Texas Longhorns t-shirt of mine looks good on you. But I think we need to update your wardrobe. After Sierra's off to school, we'll head into town and get you some new clothes, not thrift store finds."

Images popped into Faith's mind of boutiques, each lined with racks of dresses and outfits, shoes, and accessories. Colors, patterns, styles, and brands, she could almost feel the textures beneath her fingertips. She could see helpful sales associates who carried merchandise for her to the fitting room, all potential purchases if she liked them. She remembered no faces or names, but she knew it was part of her past.

She pictured leaving with boxes and bags of goodies. So many images popped into her mind, she knew she had frequently shopped at nice stores. She smiled at Colby. "That would be good." Finally, something would be familiar.

"We can take my old Wagoneer." Colby pointed to the age-worn, large vehicle to the left.

Faith examined the two options. She and Colby stood on the porch, watching Sierra's school bus faded into a cloud of red dust. The other choice seemed to be a vintage-aged pickup truck. "Don't you own a car?" Something without rust as the dominate color?

He cracked a grin. "Now what good is a car on a ranch? Can't haul and can't carry much with it. It won't make it into the fields or woods when it's rough. In fact, can't do much at all with a car." Shaking his head, he took her hand and led her to the passenger side of the Jeep. He opened her door, and it took Faith a moment to realize his chivalrous intent. Blushing, she slid in. She was startled to see he kept the key dangling in the ignition. The engine started with a coughing grunt, and Colby patted the dash affectionately.

"These beasts have served me well. Sierra likes to drive this one."

"She's only seven!"

"Well, she's got to sit on my lap to see out and my knees hit the dash so she can reach the pedals, but one day she'll be able to say her old man had her driving his old truck across the fields where she grew up."

It was a sweet image, and coupled with Colby's lolling tone, stirred something deep inside Faith's chest. A memory knocked and she gripped the armrest trying to force it to the surface of her mind.

"Don't try so hard. They'll come when they're ready to."

She spun to face him, startled at his gentle suggestion. He grinned. "Your face was squished up like when Sierra is thinking really hard."

They turned off Colby's dirt road onto another dirt road, which led to yet another dirt road. They passed four tractors, numerous barns, endless trucks, six people on horseback, miles of fence and fields, and only one car. Laundry flapped in yards. Flags snapped from poles. Dogs sprawled on porches. Livestock was everywhere.

"What are those white boxes?"

"Beehives. Some folks keep bees for the honey and wax."

Faith massaged her temples for a moment. Would she ever find her previous life again? Why did everything around her seem so foreign?

"Are you okay?"

"Umm, just starting with a headache. Trying too hard, I suppose." She studied his profile, an appealing blend of patience and strength. "How did Sierra get her nickname Button?"

His face split into a big smile. "I used to say I wish I had a pause button with her. Five more minutes to enjoy those special moments. Her first smile, first walk, first words. Later, her first hug, bike ride, and that first time she came to me to fix her world. Over time, it just stuck." He swallowed and coughed once before finishing. He cut her a bashful grin. "I wish I could hit the pause button on these years with her now, so she never had to grow up."

"I think that is beautiful, Colby." Faith reached across the space separating them and rested her hand on his arm, feeling warmth. And sizzle. His blue gaze flicked to her, surprised, and he turned to the road, blinking rapidly.

They reached town, and a sign heralded Welcome to Crazy Woman. She scoffed, feeling very crazy at moments. More flags fluttered from porches and storefronts. Trucks of every size lined the streets. They rolled through two stop signs and one blinking yellow light and one traffic light.

"How many people live here?"

"In town? Around eight hundred last censuses. Henderson County has almost three times that many."

Faith hoped they never all came to town on the same day. It could be disastrous.

"Reckon we should check with the sheriff first, just to see if anyone has filed a missing person report on you." He stopped the truck in front of the building and a sign heralding County Sheriff, and he came around to Faith's side. He took her hand into his as she climbed out.

"Do you think they would? File a report?"

He looked her up and down. "Minus your scuffs, you look like you stepped off the pages of some hoity-toity fashion magazine. Stands to reason someone, somewhere would be looking for you." He stroked a thumb along her cheek. "I sure would if I lost you."

Fifteen minutes later, they left the police station. Faith's shoulders slumped as she trudged down the steps. No one reported her missing. No one was looking for her. Except for Colby, it felt like no one cared she was gone. Had she always been this unwanted?

Colby's warm hand rested on her shoulder, and she stopped, turning to meet his broad smile. The twinkling in his eyes stilled her heart.

"Looks like we'll have to get you that new wardrobe now. Appears you'll be staying on just a bit longer."

She caught the joy in his voice, and she smiled. As they fell into step, she leaned her head against his shoulder and his arm dropped to her waist, bringing her close. She smelled his musky scent and cinnamon. For now, it felt good to be desired.

The click of his boots on the sidewalk mirrored the lighter step of her new shoes. He slowed his natural swinging gait to accommodate her tighter one. She silently questioned why she walked the way she did. She had only the slightest sway to her hips, her steps were measured and felt almost stunted. She instinctively knew it had more to do than just her bruises and aches.

She couldn't find an answer to her gait in the recesses of her mind, so she focused on their walk down the street, passing various shop windows and stores all dressed for Christmas with gay decorations, lights, and more. They turned a few corners, leaving the police station and their truck far behind them. She was hopelessly lost, but it was alright. Colby would keep her safe.

It warmed her inside to feel wanted by the big, rugged rancher. And protected.

"Here we go. We should be able to get you properly outfitted in here."

They stopped in a parking lot, at a store that towered over the parking lot. Faith stared at the sign, wondering if he were joking. What did he expect her to wear from here? Perhaps she'd misread him terribly. With a heavy heart that chased away her earlier contentment, she followed him into the Tractor Supply store.

Colby stood, hands in his pockets and a frown furrowing his brow. He'd never shopped for women's clothes before and now he was doing it a second time in as many days. This time, Faith was along, so he couldn't screw it up too bad. Even without memories, she had to know how to shop. He knew lots of wives and girlfriends who shopped here, and they always looked nice.

Right now, he was so nervous, he hoped she didn't

notice his shaking. He'd been so scared they had a missing report filed with the police and she would be whisked away, back to whoever left those bruises on her. He prayed all night that would not be the case, but he knew he had to do the right thing and check in with the law. For now, it seemed like she was meant to be with him and Sierra, and he aimed to enjoy every moment he was given with her.

He'd meant what he said about looking for her if he lost her. He'd said those words to comfort her, since she looked like she was going to cry right then. And he meant them. For the life of him, he couldn't understand why there wasn't a state-wide all-points bulletin for her, especially since there had been a ring on her finger recently.

Touching her cheek was like stroking the softest silk. Her skin reminded him of rose petals. Shame it was winter; he'd love to pluck a rose or two and spend some time taking a petal at a time and caressing her satiny skin.

He'd almost burst into tears when she asked him about Button's nickname. He still had no clue how he was going to counter the custody suite, but he wasn't losing his little girl. He needed to stop chasing stray cattle and go talk to a lawyer. As soon as things with Faith settled down, he'd go.

He scrubbed his hands along his jeans and then reached for Faith's hand, shooting her a wink. "Ready for some fun?" Her less-than-enthusiastic return made him laugh. "Come on, honey." He led the charge over to the women's apparel.

The yellow cotton sundress caught his eye first. She'd set him on fire by wearing that. He told himself though it was December, but she could wear it while sitting by a crackling fireplace, and if wishes came true, she'd light up his days when warm weather returned in a few months. He grabbed one off the rack and held it up to her for size. Recklessly, he added two more and looked around for the fitting rooms.

"You try those on for size, and I'll scout around for some more stuff." He gave her a gentle shove. "Wrangler and Carhartt. We'll be all set." He clapped his hands together with a satisfied sweep.

An hour later, Colby slid his credit card across the point-of-sale machine as two clerks bagged their purchases. He signed his name with a flourish and sent Faith another joyful wink. He couldn't wait to get her out of those granny clothes and into something nice enough to make him drool. And he would take that whole batch right back to the thrift store and donate them. She'd tried to get into the spirit of shopping, but he could tell most of it was forced for his benefit. That made him appreciate her more for her attempt.

She was now the reluctant owner of that hot little yellow sundress sold at an out of season discount. She also had a thick, layered denim skirt, and a sexy long silk blue crinkly skirt. For shirts she had a nice selection of both long sleeve and short sleeve t-shirts, a pink camo sweatshirt, and five more graphic designed sweatshirts, two pretty sweaters in stripes of blue and green, some ladies' rancher blouses, and two warm coats of varying weights.

She had enough jeans to last a week that cradled her pretty little backside and a truck load of accessories. He watched as they bagged up her leather belt, and a small handbag, plus a pretty silver pendant necklace that he caught her looking at, and he scooped it up into the pile before she could object. Once he found her correct shoe size, he added butt-kicking boots in turquoise and brown and a pair of pink camo moccasin slippers to wear around the house. Unable to resist, he'd topped the purchases off with lacy bras, one in white and a matching one in pink. He added socks, and bikini underwear that would feed his fantasies.

She'd fought him over pajamas, saying he'd spent more than enough on her, and she was fine with using his Longhorns t-shirt. Unable to deny how mouth-watering good she looked in it, he relented. For now.

Each loaded down like pack mules, they headed to the door. A window ad caught his eye. "Look at that. The Christmas Founder's Day Dance is this Saturday. And lucky you've got plenty of clothes to pick from now." He sent her a flirty wink. "Can you save me a few dances?"

CHAPTER **FIVE**

On Friday night Colby and Jack rode their horses into the barn and untacked them. They were both cold and tired and hungry, but all the cattle were accounted for and moved into the south pasture for the rest of the winter.

"I'm so hungry, I could eat a bear."

Colby snickered, though he could echo his friend's sentiment. "Lucky for the bears, they're all hibernating. You might have to settle for a steer."

Jack slung the saddle over his shoulder and took it to the bench. "I am so tired of smelling cows. I sure don't want to eat one now. What's your pretty filly, Faith, cooking up?"

Colby set his saddle next to Jack's and hung the bridle up above it. Heat coursed through him, and he disguised it by snatching up a dandy brush and applying it to his horse's hindquarters. "She ain't my filly, and I have no idea what she's fixing. Whatever she feels like, I reckon."

"Uh huh." Jack put a final brushstroke along his gelding's neck and tossed the brush back in the bucket. He led the horse to its stall and checked the hay net and water bucket. He returned for Colby's mount while Colby busied himself by grabbing a pail and filling it with oats. Like a well-oiled machine, the two men worked silently tending to the stock. Each time they passed in the aisle, Jack smirked, and Colby felt his neck burn in embarrassment.

Once all the horses were tended to, they pulled the big barn doors closed. Colby looked at the house, where the lights burned invitingly. Admittedly, it warmed his heart, knowing Sierra and Faith were waiting inside.

He turned to Jack. "How did we run this place when one of us had to stay behind and watch Sierra?"

"I did the work of two men."

Colby scoffed at Jack's glib remark. "In your dreams, dude."

They peeled off their gloves as they reached the side door and slammed to a halt. Surprised, they quietly stole along the hall, following the giggles and merry holiday tunes. They reached the living room, and stood, transfixed by the view. All thoughts of cold and hunger fled from Colby's mind as Jack slipped his hand on his shoulder and leaned close to whisper.

"If you don't claim her as your gal, partner, I sure will."

The tree stood resplendent in countless bulbs, angels, and assorted decorations. Tinsel and garland stretched along the walls, and a glittery family of deer graced the mantel above where the fire crackled. Giant nutcrackers stood sentinel on either side of the fireplace glowing in the firelight and candles flickered everywhere, lending a romantic hint to the scene of holly berries, greenery, and twinkling lights. Succulent roast beef scents wafted in from the kitchen. Carols played softly on the radio.

At the heart of the holiday display filling his living

room sat Sierra and Faith. Their backs were turned to him and Jack, and Colby felt like a spy, but he was unable to move away. Sierra leaned her head against Faith's shoulder and Faith had his arm around his daughter's shoulder. The sight was so beautiful, tears came to Colby's eyes.

"I'm so glad you agreed to decorate, Faith. It takes Daddy forever to do this, and I just love how pretty it looks."

"It does look nice, and I am happy to do this with you. I had a wonderful time."

Sierra giggled. "Me too. Daddy never puts up all these extra things."

Colby and Jack exchanged guilty looks. True, Colby mentally acknowledged his daughter's words. They just put up a few things, never emptying the boxes. Sierra and Faith must have not left one decoration behind. Truth was, Colby forgot they had most of those things, like the deer family and all those candles.

"Well, sweetie, they're up now. I just hope the men like them."

Sierra inhaled as if surprised. "Are you kidding? They'll love them. I can't wait for them to get here."

"Me too. I'd better go check that beef roast before they do arrive. The vegetables should be done soon. I'll put the rolls in now. No doubt they'll be hungry."

Faith started to rise. Jack yanked Colby backward and they quietly moved outside and eased the door closed.

"Never reckoned we'd walk in on that scene," Jack said as he rubbed his jaw.

"Me neither. What are we gonna do?"

"We're gonna walk in like it's our first time. We'll notice

the room and tree for the first time. And we never heard a thing."

Trust Jack to know what to do. Colby shook, overcome with emotions. The room was pretty enough, but seeing his daughter and Faith side by side, nestled close, and overhearing their conversation… he could barely think. "Jack…"

"Colby, pull yourself together. You can handle this. But I'm warning you, you'd better lay claim to Faith before I do."

Colby nodded slowly and drew in a deep breath. "Too late. As Sierra says, finders keepers. I found her; I'm keeping her."

Jack punched his arm. "We might see about that. Let's go. I'm still hungry."

Saturday morning, and they feasted on a breakfast of bacon and eggs with buttermilk biscuits and gravy. Faith felt impressed with herself as she rolled out the dough Colby had prepared and baked the biscuits. She also made the thick gravy, with a little help from Sierra. She was slowly adjusting to the kinds of food they prepared and ate. Something told her bacon and sawmill gravy had never been on her menu before. However, she found herself liking certain aspects of the foods and what felt like a new sensation of getting her hands dirty in the cooking.

Afterward, Colby helped Faith clear the table. He carried a stack of plates into the kitchen where she was already filling the sink with hot water and a few squirts of dish soap.

"Just leave them all to soak, honey. We can wash them later."

Lemon scent lifted into the air. Faith tried to pretend she hadn't noticed his subtle endearment. "Why?"

"The sooner we get to town, the soon we can celebrate." His smile was huge. He took the last two skillets and slid them into the sink. "Now, go get ready. Dress for a day that's mostly outside, so your heavier jacket, and inside with lots of activities tonight."

She stared at her reflection in the mirror Colby had installed in her room. She wore her hair down, clean and combed straight, a color block cable sweater of green hues that accented her curves, form-fitting blue jeans, and the turquoise and brown cowboy boots. She topped off the look with a light coat of berry lip glass.

While she could see she looked attractive, the clothes did not feel right. Almost like she was trying to wear a man's suit and pass it off as hers. These might fit her physically, but they were not hers at a subconscious level. She gazed deep into the dark brown eyes looking back at her—the eyes of a stranger—and wondered what secrets her silent conscious was keeping.

"Hard to say," she muttered. She would bet Colby's ranch that whatever she saw today at the Christmas celebration would surprise her.

"Faith? We're waiting on you." Colby's yell echoed through the house.

Since she wasn't sure what else she could do to prepare, she slipped from the room. Colby met her in the hallway. He already had her jacket ready.

"Your chariot awaits, my lady." His eyes sparkled in merriment, and he extended his arm, bowing slightly. Sierra copied his movement, a huge grin on her happy face. A giggle rose in Faith's throat as she wrapped her arm around

Colby's and warmth crackled between them as he led her out to where Jack waited beside the newest of the two old trucks. Her chariot.

It wasn't just a Christmas dance, Faith quickly realized, it was an entire day of holiday celebration. Colby, Sierra, Jack, and herself left the ranch shortly after breakfast, riding in Colby's old Jeep. Jack and Sierra laughed and joked in the back while she and Colby joined in when they could.

Parking was hard to come by once they reached town. Faith studied the long rows of vehicles, mostly pickup trucks, and longer rows of people standing around, and she shook her head in amazement. Many of the trucks had decorations of banners, wreaths, and Grinches attached. There was not a single sleek car in sight. The hickory scent of barbeque hung in the air.

"Has the entire county population come into town?"

Her question, though serious, earned hearty laughs from Colby and Jack. Colby finally found a spot big enough for his truck and they all piled out. Jack rushed to take Faith's arm.

"Ma'am, may I?" he said as he slid his arm through hers and passed Colby a sneer.

She giggled at the thin-lip snarl Colby gave Jack and then allowed herself to be escorted away. Colby picked up Sierra and rushed to catch up.

They only traveled a short distance, and Jack let out a merry hoot and led Faith toward loud music and raucous laughter. Colorful booths lined the street, now shut off by police barriers. Flags fluttered in the cool air. Songs blared over mounted speakers. People lined up, traveling from booth to booth, trying their luck to win prizes. Lucky contestants walked away carrying stuffed snowmen, portly penguins, silly Santas, and round reindeer.

"Games! Daddy, win me a stuffed toy."

"I think Uncle Jack is the game expert, honey. He has a much better chance at winning you a prize than me."

Smooth as honey, Colby slid up and took Faith's free arm and looked pointedly at Jack, who gave her a regretful pat. "I'll be back, ma'am."

"That was slick, mister," Faith said with a chuckle as Jack took Sierra to the booth of her choice. She looked up at Colby and basted in his satisfied smile. "Are you two always so competitive?"

"Sometimes." Colby traced her jaw with his index finger. "When the prize is worth it."

She inhaled, taking in the cold air through her nostrils. It served to cool her thoughts as she stared into Colby's deep eyes. She glanced around, studied Jack and Sierra as they stood at another booth. People moved all around them, laughing and rushing, oblivious to the incredible way Colby warmed her with just a smile and a touch.

She licked her lips and gathered her thoughts. "What else is there to do at this…?" Festival? Party? Event? Images swam through her mind of lavish houses, manicured gardens, formal gowns, tuxedos, fine drinks, and even better food. She knew she had attended grand parties that shared nothing in common with this small-town street event. But who had she attended them with? And where were they located at? Texas? That didn't seem right.

"Lots of stuff. They should be getting the pie-eating and weightlifting contests going soon. And—are you alright?" Noticing her silence, Colby stopped, concern making his eyes grow dark.

Guilt nudged Faith. She rushed to put on a smile. "Yes, I'm fine. You were saying?"

He gently chided her. "Faith, this might be different from what you're used to, but this is what you're making memories of now." He tipped her chin up and dropped a butterfly kiss on her nose.

The kiss was sweet, honest, and tender. She drew away and nodded. "You're right." She blinked at the moisture in her eyes created by his tenderness. She took his hand in hers. "Let's go make some memories."

Colby wrapped his arm around Faith as the tractors chugged down the road. John Deeres, International Harvesters, Farmalls, and New Hollands rolled along, bedecked with lights, ribbons, garland, and wreaths, Drivers waved, some dressed in Santa suits, and family members walked along, tossing out candy to the cheering crowd.

An elf traveling with Santa driving a Farmall tractor tossed a handful of candy toward Sierra. She squealed, broke from Faith's grip, and rushed out into the street to claim it.

"Sierra, no!" Faith leapt forward and called her back.

"Easy, Faith, she's all right." Colby murmured in her ear as he tightened his hold on her waist. Once more he was struck with the suspicion she came from a bigger, more dangerous world. One where children wouldn't be allowed to run into a parade street. Where had she come from? Who was still there, waiting to hear from her? He slid a glance at her left hand, to the pale white circle. His chest compressed and he sucked in a breath. Where was the man who gave her the ring? Was it the same one who left multiple bruises on her?

Sierra returned, both her fists full of wrapped candy. She proudly held up her hands. "Faith, pick one."

Colby watched as she started to protest, looked up at him, and then smiled at Sierra.

"Thank you. That is kind of you," she said, plucking one bright red foil candy from Sierra's hand. "I think this one is so pretty."

Sierra beamed and Colby felt like a mule kicked him as he watched the tender exchange.

"It came from Santa, but I know he's not the real Santa Clause. He lives around here and is just pretending his tractor's a sleigh and he's Santa."

Faith did a grand job of acting surprised and Colby bit back a laugh. Jack chortled and plucked a blue foil candy from Sierra's hand.

"Lil' Miss is a smart cookie," Jack praised, unwrapped the candy and tossed it in his mouth.

Colby's gaze met Faith's and they shared a smile. Something in her tender gaze reached out and touched his heart.

"Oh, look! Horses!" Sierra exclaimed, pointing frantically at the first row of horses clip clopping along next in the parade. Horses of every color, their rider's just as colorful in their holiday outfits pranced along, their heads bobbing and sleigh bells ringing. Carolers followed alongside, singing 'Jingle Bells' to the musicians behind them.

"Never mind we have horses at the ranch," Colby whispered in Faith's ear. "These are prettier because they're decked out in bells, lights, and costumes."

She grinned and leaned close. "Maybe you should put a Santa costume and bells on her horse?"

He laughed at that.

Next came the school kids, tweens up to high schoolers. Each group wore bright red and green outfits, and marched along, showcasing their unique talents. Young tweens tumbled and did backflips and handstands. Older tweens danced and kicked. High School kids walked in step to their horns and drums. Spectators cheered and shouted at their favorite child when they marched past.

Colby gently tugged Faith away from the sidewalk. Jack and Sierra followed behind.

"Why are we leaving?" Faith asked.

"The parade is winding down. The pie eating, log splitting and various judging events will be next. We don't want to miss them."

"No, we wouldn't want that."

Colby chuckled at her dry, disbelieving remark.

CHAPTER SIX

Faith felt like she'd landed in a foreign land. Everyone around her seemed to act like this was a normal part of life, but she was sure she'd never seen anything like this before. She would not think it so odd if she had. The gaiety, laughter, pageantry of the parade, the colors and sounds around her, all of it seemed so unknown. She saw Christmas trees of every height, decorated in every imaginable theme and lights hanging in every conceivable place. People dressed in red and green with hats, vests, sweaters, boots, scarves and more. Many sported silly accessories like flashing necklaces of Christmas bulbs or deer antler headbands or blinking jewelry. Endless merry holiday greetings from each passing person assured her it was unquestionably Christmas time. As did the cool air sometimes blowing down her back. She knew the ground should be white with snow, but it wasn't.

Vague memories nipped at her, like the cold breeze, images of snow piled in dirty white mountains or falling like stardust beneath dazzling lights. Here, in Crazy

Woman, Henderson County, Texas, there was no snow. No one else seemed to notice or mind the ground was green. Where did she normally spend Christmas? Pictures flashed through her mind, too fast to grab.

Darn amnesia. Her jaw clenched and she balled her fists in frustration. Simple thing: where did she spend Christmas?

"Faith?"

Colby's gentle call brought her back and she blinked back a tear. "I'm sorry."

He squeezed her hand. "Don't force it. They'll come when they're ready to."

They were her memories. She was ready now. Didn't that account for something?

She sensed that while she had patience, she was not used to being kept waiting.

Colby's smile was warm and soft, his eyes tender. Her insides warmed like honey and thoughts of lost memories faded. He traced his calloused fingertip down her nose, a playful gesture she'd seen him do with Sierra. She exhaled, slowly letting a long breath out, and gave him a nod. Whatever this bizarre day may hold, she would be okay.

Hours later, they stopped at a bench. Faith and Sierra plopped down and exchanged exhausted giggles. Colby sat down beside her and brushed his thigh against hers. Even through the rough denim he wore, she felt a sizzling thrill at their touch.

"I am so hungry," Sierra exclaimed.

Colby harrumphed, coughing into his palm. "Don't see

how that's possible with all the cookies, cocoa, and pie you ate."

"I cannot imagine one more thing squeezed into this day." Faith added. "I've never seen anyone eat so much pie so fast as those people back at the table. That young man certainly earned his blue ribbon, though I don't see how he will be able to look at a pumpkin for weeks."

"The dance is the culmination of the day." Jack checked his watch. "It ought to begin in about an hour or so." He reached out and pulled Sierra to her feet and took her by the shoulders. His gaze landed pointedly on Colby. "Reckon I'll take the little lady. And. Get. Her. Some. Dinner."

"Huh? Oh, yeah, right. Dinner. Uh, Sierra, you go with Uncle Jack, and he'll rustle you some grub."

"What about you and Faith?"

He smiled at his daughter. "Don't you worry. We'll be just fine. You run along now, honey. I love you and I'll see you later."

As he stood up, Jack leaned in. "Abe Duckett is giving us a ride back to the ranch."

Colby nodded. "Thanks, pal. I owe you one."

Jack grinned. "Don't you always?"

"Competitive, but devoted to one another," Faith observed as Jack and Sierra walked away. "There's probably nothing he wouldn't do for you."

Colby grinned. "Except maybe never apologize for bloodying my nose in first grade. That was our first introduction to one another." He reached for her arm. "Shall we go find some dinner ourselves before the dance starts?"

"Alright." She climbed to her feet. "What do you have in mind?"

"Dimples? It's a nice little diner two blocks over. They

specialize in breakfast and lunches, but their dinners are good too. They have some great hot sandwiches and blue-plate specials."

Dimple's. What an odd name for a restaurant. She had no clue what hot sandwiches or blue plates might be, still, Colby liked it. "Lead the way." She gave a good-hearted sigh and followed him. Her sigh turned to delighted surprise as he smoothly slipped his hand around hers.

Hands linked they walked along the sidewalk to Dimple's Diner. Citizens moved around them, some shopping and carrying parcels, others tugging tired children, and some wandering slowly and taking in the sights and sounds and smells of the area. Faith's intake was overstimulated, and the music piping from the stores was adding to her hyperalert state. She was looking forward to a sit-down time with Colby, to be alone and decompress from the day.

Dimple's Diner was full by the time they arrived, and Colby spotted a table along the back. "It will be quieter here than up front," he promised as he guided her onto the smooth booth seat.

"You are such a gentleman, Colby."

He looked startled at her observation. "A man ought to treat a lady like she's a precious gem."

Faith tried to think of something to reply, but in truth, his honest remark left her stunned. She had a feeling she'd not been someone's precious gem. But what about the man who gave her the missing ring? Her gaze drifted to the faint white circle on her finger before rising to meet Colby's face. He offered her a menu, a two-sided card, typed and decorated with thumbnail photos of food and laminated. Breakfast on one side, lunch and dinner on the other.

"The soup looks good." She placed her chipped fingernail on the photo of the creamy soup.

The server came and took their orders. She propped her chin on her upturned palms, elbows on the table.

"Tell me about you and Jack. It sounds like your friendship started out rocky."

Colby chuckled as he stirred sugar into his sweet tea. "We met in first grade. Jack moved to town from McAllen, a South Texas town in Hidalgo County. He punched me in the nose at recess for saying something he didn't like. Neither one of us can remember what it was now. We ended up sitting in the principal's office the rest of the day and left school that day as best friends. Been that way ever since."

"How wonderful. What a fun story."

"After a bit, folks started taking to calling us the Cheese Brothers, as in the Colby Jack cheese."

She giggled. "That's good."

"Jack's always been an old soul, even when he was young. When I bought the Tica, I asked him to be my foreman. He was my best man when I married Lucy, too. Jack's always been a part of my life, and Sierra's. She's never known a time without her Uncle Jack."

"She obviously thinks much of him."

Colby nodded, studying her as she contemplated adding cream or sugar to her coffee. In the end, she opted to drink it black.

"What about you, Faith? Do you feel you have a bff out there, someone who has your back and knows your secrets but won't tell?"

Listening to Colby describe a perfect friend, she searched her heart, hoping for a spark that would tell her someone out there cared for her like a sister. Or perhaps her best friend was a sister? Cousin? Anyone? She just felt an empty void where faces should be.

In resignation, she leaned back in her seat. "I don't believe so."

Colby leaned forward, pushed his drink aside and reached for her hand. His roughened thumbs caressed her knuckles. His eyes darkened. He licked his lips. "Faith, I don't know your secrets, and I wouldn't share if I did, but I will have your back. I won't let anyone hurt you."

Her breath hitched and she stared at him, weighing the truth of his words. Finally, she answered him. "I believe you."

Their dinners arrived, chicken parmesan for her and barbeque pulled pork for him. Colby studied their plates. "A bottle of wine would go with this nicely."

"Dimple's doesn't seem the kind of place to offer wines." Instinctively, she knew she liked wine. Dry wine. Perhaps a bottle of Barolo or Sangiovese. How could she know those names but have no memories of what they were? Wine. That was it. How utterly frustrating. Beneath the table, she stomped her foot, keeping it quiet so not to alert Colby. She hid her frustrated frown behind the coffee cup.

He chuckled, blue eyes crinkling in the corners. "No," he agreed, "but they do have fantastic pie."

Faith felt out of place—yet again. Her heart throbbed as she took in the sights before her. Red and green flags waved in the snappy wind around the big red barn, heralding the Christmas Founder's Day Dance. White lights sparkled from around the doorway and twirled up tree trunks. Small evergreen trees stuck in galvanized buckets lined the path to the barn. Strings of white lights draped the trees.

Now in twilight, they cast a merry glow against the gathering darkness.

Dinner and a shared slice of pumpkin pie was done. She'd enjoyed the playful way Colby teased her with the whipped cream as they worked their way through the pie. He had the nicest smile. And when he reached across their table and swiped a dab of whipped cream away from her upper lip with his thumb, she warmed.

"You're growing a mustache, Faith."

Unable to stop, she giggled, utterly amused by his goofy grin, which made him chuckle, which caused her to laugh more.

Now that was behind them, and she felt like a foreigner —again. Inside, where her stubborn memories lay buried, she knew this was new. She had no idea what to expect inside the big barn.

"Ready?"

She glanced up at Colby, and his hopeful smile, blue eyes crinkling, lifted something inside her. Her heart skipped a few beats, then raced ahead. Whatever her misgivings, he managed to erase them with just a look.

"Yes, I am." She exhaled, linked her arm through his, and let him escort her down the path of twinkling Christmas trees planted in buckets and decorated in various themes.

Inside the barn sat rows of tables laden with platters of snacks and drinks. Rows of chairs rimmed the walls. Pine scented the air from the trees in buckets. Five men stood on the center stage, each one holding a musical instrument. Faith identified the violin and the tall cello. She knew them! A memory poked her. Another stage, adorned with heavy curtains and lights. Men in tuxes instead of overalls and blue jeans. Women in fine gowns and heels instead of denim and boots. Hushed tones instead of hearty laughter and handshakes.

The first squeal of the violin made her jump.

"Don't worry about it."

She turned up to Colby. "What?"

"Whatever has your pretty brow all wrinkled?" Gently, he smoothed his thumb over her eyebrows, then smiling as he cupped her chin in his warm fingers. His touch was as soft as his words. "Let's have some fun."

"Okay, folks, we'll get this party started with some do-sa-do." The center stage man spoke into his microphone. "I'm ready to call this dance, so grab your partner, form your squares, and promenade right those pretty gals."

Faith froze. She understood none of what he just said. "I can't do this." She watched as couples paired up and filled the floor. Boot heels stomped the wooden floorboards and people clapped to the merry of the music.

Colby's hands slid into hers. "Sure, you can. I'll be beside you every step of the way. Long John is a great square dance caller. Just hold my hand." Crossing the floor, they joined three other couples. Colby smiled and nodded at them, addressing them by name. He pressed her palm down over his upturned palm and tenderly joined her other hand in his. The position felt strange, but she closed her eyes and drew comfort from the contact. Other musical instruments joined in, creating a lively harmony. She gave the other people a tense smile. Her stomach dipped. She was going to do this.

"Bow to your partner, your corner too." Long John sang.

Colby turned and bowed to Faith. "Watch me," he whispered as he swiveled and bowed to the woman beside him. She quickly did likewise to the man beside her.

The musicians played a tune she did not recognize but it was catchy. Long John—the caller on the stage—sang what was doubtlessly the lyrics in a gravel-rough voice, interjecting calls to move.

"Circle left, then stop at home," Long John called, and Colby took her hand and led her in a left circle along with the other three pairs of dancers until they returned to their starting point.

"Send the girls to the middle, star through, and roll away to a half sashay."

Not understanding any of the steps, she followed his lead, swinging around at the end of his extended arm. Sometimes she, and the other three ladies in their square, were handed off to the man to their left or right, depending how the caller ordered the step. Each new maneuver always led her back to Colby.

"Heads, pass through, everyone flutter the wheel, and then allemande right."

Faith panicked, not recognizing a thing Long John just sang. She sought Colby. He stood, his gaze holding hers, as his two main fingers acted out the steps. Bit by bit, and step by step, the dance unfolded. Faith followed Colby's directions, and when she was twirled or turned away from him, she followed the lead of the other ladies in their square. The other dancers were patient and helped her along with words of encouragement and quick directions. Their warm smiles and genuine enjoyment of the dance gave Faith the assurance to keep parading, twisting, and spinning.

"Allemande left, do a right left grand, reach your lady, and wrong way promenade her home."

The hand and body placement changed constantly, as Long John rasped out his calls. Allemande right, left circle, right grand, and many more. Colby guided Faith into circles, half circles, rapid turnarounds, head-spinning turns, and endless strutting. At last, the call ended, and he escorted her to a chair.

"Water?"

Breathless, she nodded, grateful at his concern. Another dance started and Colby suggested a break. He chatted with friends, introducing her as his acquaintance, with his hand resting comfortably on her knee.

"We can take a break until you're ready to go again."

She wasn't sure she'd be ready. "None of the dance moves make sense," she confided, her voice low.

He shook his head. "Don't worry. You're doing fine. Square dancing takes a bit to learn."

The tenderness in his blue eyes spoke of honesty. She had the suspicion receiving honestly was a new experience. What kind of person came from a background that did not even have basic honesty? She was beginning to wonder not only where she came from, but what kind of person she was, too.

"How does everyone else know what to do?"

"Square dancing is like any other form of dance. We all took lessons and get together to practice." He tipped his index finger along her nose. "And practice makes pretty good."

She frowned. "I don't think that's how that maxim goes."

He shrugged. "Close enough."

"Okay dokey, folks. It's time for the chicken shuffle!"

Long John made his happy announcement and people clapped and cheered. Couples who had been resting jumped up and got into long lines. Groups of young men lined up on one end of the floor and young women lined up along the other.

"What is going on?"

"You will like this dance." Colby stood and reached for her arm, gently bringing her up. "There are no precise steps. It's just moving to what feels good."

"It's the chicken shuffle!" Long John reminded the group. "Chickens strut to the left, and they strut to the right."

Moving as one, everyone tucked their hands to their hips as if imitating chicken wings and first turned one step to their left, and then one step to their right, grinning and giggling at their neighbors.

"Chickens scratch the ground."

They all scratched the floor with one foot. Then they scratched with the other. Some bent over as if pecking the floor.

"Chickens flap their wings."

Hands still on their hips, they fanned their arms, laughing.

"Chickens shake their tail feathers."

Hilarity ensued, as people shook their bottoms, extended their butts, and waggled gleefully. The kids were by far the most animated, exaggerating each chicken action and laughing gleefully,

"Almost done. Guys, roosters crow."

The men stretched up, crowing a proud "cock-a-doodle-do" cry. Faith laughed at Colby's arm flapping, neck stretching imitation of a rooster.

"And ladies, y'all lay an egg."

Faith froze. Colby laughed and pointed to some women

in front of them. The girls and ladies all squatted a moment, let loose with a pleased "ba-gock!" and shook their tail feathers.

"I think y'all got it! Here goes the chicken shuffle. Strut to the left, then strut to the right. Scratch the ground and flap your wings. Shake those tail feathers, folks!"

Faith could not help herself. She laughed until her sides ached. They all pranced around the room in big circles, stopping to scratch and flap and change direction to strut a new pattern.

"Ladies, y'all lay an egg and fellas, you crow loud and proud."

Colby looked just as ridiculous as everyone else did. And doubtlessly, she looked just as silly. "This is so fun!" she exclaimed, fresh peals of laughter escaping after she laid her egg, and another tail feather shake was called for and Colby exaggerated his 'tail' and gave a good shake. The man already had a wonderful 'tail' and didn't need to inflate its size.

Finally, the chicken shuffle was done, and the caller asked for a break for himself and the band. Colby guided Faith to a pair of chairs and eased her into one. He brought her fresh water, and one for himself.

"That was wonderfully fun," she exclaimed. "I never dreamed something with such a silly name could be so enjoyable."

"I hope you're enjoying more than just the shuffle, Faith."

"I am. This whole evening has been unbelievable. I had no idea what to expect, and I was a little apprehensive, but to be honest, I am truly enjoying myself."

"That's good, because Long John has promised a few slow waltzes."

More neighbors came up to chat, and Colby introduced them all. There was no way Faith was going to keep them all straight, or remember their names later, but one thing was clear; Each person respected Colby and treated her with equal regard, albeit with some curiosity. She sensed respect was something she knew and understood well; however, she wasn't sure she always had favor like Colby had among his peers. Just because she recognized high regard didn't assure her that she experienced it personally. Again, she had to wonder what kind of person she might be to not be respected among her equals.

Long John called for another square dance. "Folks, we're gonna dance this one to an old familiar song, Jingle Bells. Let's square up everyone." The band started the first notes of Jingle Bells.

Colby lifted an eyebrow. "This ought to be fun. Do you feel up to another dance?"

She could not say no to his hopeful grin. "Sure, why not?" She allowed him to take her out on the floor, and they met up with the same dancers they had before and lined up to form another big square while the band played in the background. She glanced around and saw a number of young children and teens partnering up into square groups. She also noticed grey-haired ladies and silver foxes, smiling, and tapping their feet, ready to dance.

"All right, let's dance folks. Bow to your partner, your corner too."

Faith remembered this part and bowed first to Colby and turned to the man beside her. Toes tapped while Long John sang the first couple of lines.

"Dashing through the snow, let's begin with a do-si-do, in a one-horse open sleigh, over the fields we go, promenade left and roll around to a right sashay."

Once more, Colby and her dance partners helped Faith through the moves. Faith caught herself relaxing and enjoying the dance more as she maneuvered the steps better. She glanced around at the youngest and the oldest dancers. The kids were surprisingly good, and the seniors all wore big smiles.

"Bells on bobtail ring, grab your lady and give her a swing, making spirits bright, allemande right, what fun it is to ride, and everyone weave the ring, a sleighing song tonight. Jingle bells, jingle bells, jingle all the way, do sa do to a wave, oh what fun it is to ride in a one-horse open sleigh, heads, all diamond circulate.

"A day or two ago, I thought I'd take a ride, circle to a line, and soon Miss Fanny Bright was seated by my side, three-quarter tag the line. The horse was lean and lank, forward and back, misfortune seemed his lot, spin the top, he got into a drifted bank, forward and back, and then we got upsot, and fan the top."

The song ended and Colby led Faith back to a chair and brought her another water.

"I thought that song was supposed to be the horse got into a drifted bank and we got upset. Have I been singing it wrong all these years?"

Colby shrugged. "Most likely, I do recall reading somewhere it was written originally as upsot. Maybe it was for the songwriter to keep the rhyme. I don't know. But it helps Long John with the calls."

"Who comes up with these crazy names to all those steps?"

Colby shrugged. "I have no idea. We can ask Long John. He might know. But they are genuine call names. You could travel to any square dance in any place, and the callers all use the same names, and the steps are almost all identical. So once you master them here, you can go anywhere and dance."

Somehow, Faith doubted wherever she was from had this kind of dancing. More neighbors and friends came over to visit. She soon forgot about dancing as she chatted with Colby's friends.

"Interesting no one's noticed any well-heeled strangers around," he murmured to Faith after several conversations with others and they drifted away.

"How's that interesting?"

"Makes me wonder if you're out here by yourself."

They both glanced at her left hand, their eyes slowly meeting with the question neither one seemed able to ask. Faith licked her lips. "There could be many other explanations why no one else has been noticed." Yet to be honest, she wasn't sure she liked any possibility in her mind.

He brought her left hand up and kissed it. A shiver raced up her arm, and along her back. Heady anticipation pumped through her like adrenaline. She could have closed her eyes and purred like a contented cat.

"Let's not worry about explanations and things like that now," Colby suggested. "I'd much rather dance with you again."

The musicians filtered back on stage, picked up their instruments, and shifted into a slow melody. Pairs of dancers moved out onto the floor, hugging up close to each other.

"All right, gents, grab your filly and bring her out. Here's a favorite old Texas waltz that'll have you dancing on the stars."

Colby lifted his eyebrow to Faith. "Care to dance on stardust with me?"

She couldn't think of anything else she'd rather do. And nowhere else but in his arms. On the floor, he drew her close with one arm going around her waist. Cinnamon and woodsy aftershave filled her nose. He held her hand with his free hand, linking fingers. He dropped a kiss on her lips, smiling mischievously. She grinned.

This time the kids stayed on the sidelines and the floor filled with grown dancers, and several pairs of grey-haired lovers, holding each other tight. Faith wondered how it felt to have a love that strong for so long. Did the man who gave her the missing ring intend to be her life-long lover? Was he even alive? Why wasn't she wearing the ring now?

Colby swayed to the slow rhythm. She scooted closer, leaving no room between them, and followed his lead. Gradually, she rested her head against his chest, hearing the steady beating of his heart. She closed her eyes, squeezed his hands, and smiled blissfully. If this was dancing to the stars, she only wanted a one-way ticket.

CHAPTER SEVEN

Monday, when Sierra returned from school, she took her books and a blanket outside. Curious, Faith trailed her to the side of the barn. Nestled against a hay bale and laying on the blanket, Sierra turned pages of the textbook, reading aloud to her audience of the screeching rooster they called Buster and two of the ranch dogs. Sierra's face looked so serious; Faith inched closer.

"Hello, Sierra. How was school today?" Gingerly, she sat down on another hay bale, well away from the livestock.

"Good. But I need a topic for my social studies class. It's not due until we go back to class after break, but I need to get started on it now. It's gotta be something local." She stopped flipping through pages and studied Faith. "Hey, I know. The legend! Crazy Woman Creek. That will work." The girl jumped up, dropped her books, and threw her arms around Faith. "Thank you for giving me a great idea. I need to talk to Daddy and Uncle Jack. This will be perfect." Excited, she raced away, with Buster the rooster clucking after her, its wings flapping.

Stunned, Faith turned to the panting dogs. "Well, I'm glad I was so helpful, whatever I just did." The shepherd dog barked, thumping his tail in the dirt. Faith brushed herself off, picked up Sierra's abandoned books, shook the blanket out, and continued her exploration of the ranch yard, aware the dogs now joined her. Glancing at the dogs, she had the suspicion she didn't spend much time around animals, and certainly not any time around barnyard creatures. She was about one hundred percent sure she did not end up at the Crazy Woman Creek via horseback, as Colby had originally assumed. For the hundredth time, she stared up into the sky and wondered who she was and where she came from.

"Isn't there anyone out there who can tell me?"

Honestly, she felt like she just dropped out of the sky.

"Daddy, tell me the Legend of the Crazy Woman Creek again," Sierra asked after dinner. "I need it for a school report. Uncle Jack says being over there reminds him of his ex-wives."

Faith hid her smile as she watched Colby clench his teeth, roll his eyes to the ceiling and grimace. She'd bet 'Uncle' Jack was going to have some explaining to do soon. Colby was tolerant, but only to a point when it came to his more colorful comments around Sierra.

Colby set aside his bookkeeping he'd been working on and waited for Sierra to settle next to him. "Without including Uncle Jack, tell me about this report, Button."

Soon he launched into a tale of Indians lovers, wars, and sorrow. Warm light from the Christmas tree fell over them like a soft blanket of white. Watching the two of them, the trust and adoration in little Sierra's eyes as her daddy spoke and the utter love Colby shone for his daughter gave Faith goosebumps. She rubbed her arms and inched closer to the crackling flames in the fireplace. What a beautiful, tender picture they made! She wished for a camera to capture the purity of the scene.

Her heart cracked at the innocence and magic of the moment. Had she spent time like this with her own father? She had no memories of him, or a mother or siblings. Her bottom lip quivered as Colby wove the legend like a tapestry.

"And now on certain nights you can see the maiden's footprints leading into the river. You can still hear her cries of anguish. They say she won't allow another couple to remain in love and even today will drag one of them into the river to drown them. Then the water runs red."

Faith dabbed at a tear gathered in her eye. The legend warred with the peaceful, loving scene spun around them. What a tragic ending to a sad legend. The logs hissed and spit, shooting sparks into the air.

Cicadas chirped, still defiant against the cool of the night. Colby sank deep into the rocker, letting the swallow of beer slide slowly down his throat. He set the bottle on the plank on his downward rock and eased out a long breath on the upward swing. The longer Faith stayed on, the less inclined he was to have her leave. If she ever recovered her memories and found there was another life out there somewhere. He'd read where some amnesiacs never recover their memories and just settled into new lives. He'd be okay with that. As long as she settled in at the Tica with him and Sierra.

After the night of dancing, he knew it would tear his heart out to see her pack her things and leave him. And he also knew she'd been having some flashbacks of memories lately. Nothing concrete enough to piece together, but he feared it was just a matter of time.

And there was the problem of Sierra's material grandparents wanting her. He felt the snarl form on his face just thinking about it. He'd procrastinated long enough, trying to put this on his back burner. Now he needed to face this head on. Instead of sitting back, wanting to claw the bull, he had to wade in there and grab the beast by its horns.

He needed to fight for his daughter. And for Faith. Because he couldn't stand to lose either one of them.

"Care to share what's on your mind?"

As if conjured by his thoughts, she stood before him, sexy as hell in her overall jeans, beaded slippers, and shearling jacket. Damn. He reached for his beer, and she bent, handing it to him. He grinned at the bottle in her hand. He nodded to the adjacent rocker and smiled at the picture they made, rocking on the porch, and sipping a beer. Oh, man...

"Are you okay?"

"Yeah, just a lot on my mind." Boy, wasn't that an understatement?

She took a delicate sip of beer as though it were wine in a crystal goblet. "I'll listen."

He hardly knew where to begin. He studied the evening sky, alive with colors of pink, purple, and orange.

"Have you ever wondered about the lasts in life?" he finally asked, hoping he didn't come off sounding like a wimpy sap.

"What do you mean?"

He gestured around them. "We never know the last time we get to do or see anything. The last time you toss a ball with the dog, last night out with your buddies, last sunset." He stopped, voice catching. He coughed. "Last time to see someone in their dress, the last hug, the last dance. And the last kiss."

She nodded. "Actually, yes, I have considered that. What…lasts…are behind me and I don't remember them? Only I can't bring back the emotions and memories of that last dance or kiss I might have experienced. Was it good or bad?"

She blinked and wiped her eyes. Was she crying? She had plenty to cry about. Here he was getting all sappy while she had no clue what the last time of anything was in her past. What was wrong with him lately? The evening train chugged through town, its whistle blasting in the distance.

Faith pulled a tissue from her pocket and blew her nose. He had to wonder if she kept a supply handy for when those emotional moments overwhelmed her. "Here's one I've wondered about," she said. "Why did you name your place Tica?"

A grin tugged at his lips. "When Lucy and I married, she knew I wanted to be a rancher. When Sierra was about three, we bought this place. She stuck around maybe two months. Then one day she said she'd had enough of living a lie, living out here, without any of the things I could not afford for her. Off she went, leaving us. I hadn't settled on a name for the ranch yet, and immediately thought of Tica. Things I Can't Afford."

He watched her reaction in the porch light glow. She

tilted her head to one side for a moment. Did she appreciate his satirical humor?

"Witty, but sad. Especially for Sierra. She seems to have adjusted well."

His breath caught. "She has. She barely remembers her mama. Kind of like what I imagine you're experiencing, just a few pieces here and there." He paused, pulling in a tight breath. "Lucy's parents want custody of Sierra. They haven't seen her in almost five years, but they figure they can raise her better than I can."

"What would make them think that? Particularly since they haven't seen her in so long?"

Colby took a drag of his beer and shook his head. "I don't know what bee flew into their bonnet, but they are taking me to court soon, to prove how unfit a parent I am."

She gasped, her hand going to her throat as she turned to face him square. Red stained her cheeks as she stared at him, light sparking in her eyes, reflecting off the porch glow. "Anyone who watches you with her for any length of time will easily see you are a fantastic father. I was so moved tonight as you were telling her that folklore."

"Thank you, Faith. That means a lot to me. But I am also a single parent. Her grandparents can give her a male and female parental figure." He smiled despite himself. "All I can give her is myself and Jack."

She looked out at the silhouetted barns and trees. After what seemed like a short eternity, she reached across and gripped his hand. He stopped rocking. Her expression was serious. Her voice was soft. "Maybe together, you and I could give Sierra a male and female parental figure. I could be a good mom to her."

Colby's heart took wings. His soul sang. His pulse leapt.

His mind raced. Her words were soft as feather down. They would make a fine parental team for Sierra. And she would make a great wife. And he would be a good husband.

Reality slammed into him with all the tenderness of an angry steer. He could have kissed her, but instead, he gently traced her left ring finger. Chest heavy, he fought to get the words out. "Maybe you already are."

"Faith, you seem restless tonight," Colby observed from his spot by the fire. He set his bookkeeping aside. "Would you like to go to town with Jack tomorrow? He has a handful of errands to do, and he might like the company."

Faith dropped into a chair and twirled her fingers. "I can't help it." She fought to still her hands. The fire sputtered as a log fell, sending embers shooting up the chimney. She jumped, inhaling sharply. "I don't know what's wrong with me."

Colby chuckled. "I can make a couple guesses. Relax. It's all gonna be okay. Go with Jack tomorrow and try to forget stuff for a little while."

"Are you sure you're okay with sending me with him?"

"Of course. Jack might be a bit of a conniver, but his heart is pure. And I trust you. He leaves about nine-thirty."

She stood up. "Alright. I'll be ready."

Colby climbed to his feet, laying the papers aside. "Come here," he requested, reaching out to Faith. "I want you to know, regardless of what we find out, if we ever find out, I am so happy you're here with me now. And with Sierra. She talks about you a lot more than I think you realize. Selfishly, I hope you stay on indefinitely, but I also see how the unknowns can eat at you." He cupped her chin. "Just know I am in no hurry to see you leave here."

She was about to speak, when his lips touched hers, warm and soft. His facial hair tickled her nose in the most pleasing way. His breath, scented with coffee and sweetened cream, fanned her face. His fingers dipped to her shoulders, and his calloused fingertips brushed under the neckline of her shirt and rubbed along her collarbone to her shoulders.

She reached up on tip toes to deepen the kiss and a low moan rumbled from her throat.

He slowly lifted his lips from hers. His eyes dark in the glow of the Christmas lights and crackling fire. He touched a fingertip to her lips. "Shhh. It will be okay. Good night." He turned to bank the fire and then moved purposely to the stairs. Once he was gone, and she was alone, she sank into the chair and faced the fire, the blinking lights to her left. Being honest with herself, she'd be happy to just stay here at Tica with Colby, Sierra, and Jack indefinitely, too. But she had to settle who she was first. She had to find out if she left another family out there somewhere before she could commit to this one.

CHAPTER **EIGHT**

"I sure am happy to have you riding shotgun with me, Ma'am."

Faith bounced along the front seat of Colby's truck, one hand clutching the seat fabric beside her. Jack was a much faster driver than Colby, and he seemed to know every hole in the road, since Faith was sure he hadn't missed one yet. "What makes you say that, Jack?"

"It gets you away from the ranch for a bit, gives me some fine company, and keeps you away from Colby."

He sent her a flirty wink and big smile. By now, she knew the competitiveness between the two men was harmless and mostly for their own fun. She grinned. "Don't you think Colby deserves some of my fine company?"

Jack's scowl was jealous, but still good natured. "He's got plenty." He started ticking names off on his finger, drumming the steering wheel as he went. "There's Sierra, Buster, Ben. And myself when I'm there. If he gets lonely, he can go see the cows."

Faith laughed. "You are too funny."

"If I can make you see humor and laughter, Ma'am, I've had a good day."

Town was a welcome sight for Faith. For starters, the roads were smoother. Christmas decorations still swayed in the air or brightened shopfronts. Small trees decorated in lights and tinsel, nutcracker and Santa statues, and sparkling wreaths decorated doorways and along sidewalks. Window displays held smaller statues, presents wrapped so pretty, cardinals on tree branches and more.

It was literally impossible to not feel the Christmas spirit. It infused a person's mind.

They parked along the main street, in front of the Crazy Woman Creek post office. Jack rushed over to open Faith's door. Once again, the majority of the vehicles were trucks, and a few tractors. The trucks alternated between huge, newer vehicles with big tires, protected grilles, and massive trailer hitches alongside older models with mismatched colors for doors, hoods, and beds. Most sported at least one layer of red dust, and a few hauled trailers. The fetid smells of diesel fuel, manure, and smoke exhaust filled the air. There was not one single sleek car to be found. Faith now accepted this as normal, but she knew it wasn't her normal.

Jack took Faith's arm. "We can start here. I need to pick up a package and send out a couple of letters."

They waited in line for a few minutes, then Jack withdrew two long envelopes from his jeans pocket, slid them across the counter and added a yellow slip of paper. The clerk, a large-bosomed woman in her mid-thirties, took the paper and envelopes, stepped behind the wall, and soon returned with a large box. As she hefted it onto the counter, something rattled inside. She winked at Jack.

"What ya have in there, Jack? It's heavy as a newborn calf."

"Just parts for the tractor, honey."

They exchanged banter for a minute, and then Faith followed him out. He assisted her to the seat before dropping the box in the back. Next up came the feed store.

"Hey, Nate, I need to put in an order." Jack withdrew a creased notebook page from his front pocket and unfolded it. "Grain, hay, oats, salt. It's all right here. Can you deliver next week? Maybe Tuesday?"

Nate, balding, rotund, and fiftyish, read the list over and nodded. "Shouldn't be a problem. I'll charge this to Colby's account." He paused, looking at Faith. "You must be the little lady Colby found?"

Well, at least he called her little lady, and not filly. She moved her head up and down. "Yes. That's right."

"We're calling her Faith," Jack supplied. "That's cause we're all faithful she'll decide to stick around and won't get tired of us cowpokes."

Jack and Nate both laughed at that. Next stop was the hardware store. Jack grabbed a cart at the door and produced yet another crumpled list and smoothed it out on his leg. He caught Faith's glance.

"My lists may be wadded up a mite, but I never come to town without them. And more important, I stick to my lists. All the magazines I've read say that makes me a smart shopper."

"I suppose that would be true. You are certainly organized." That surprised her about Jack. Around the ranch, he didn't always seem orderly or well-planned, but today he was showing her that side.

"See? Colby isn't the only one who is always the boy

scout. But I meant what I said before. We all do hope you plan to stay on at the Tica with us."

She stopped halfway down the hardware store aisle. Where else could she go? "Jack…" She turned to him.

"Don't worry, ma'am." He took one of her hands into his. "I didn't mean to spook you with that. I just meant once you knew who you were—if you figure out who you are—you'd still be welcome to stay on with us. Sierra would love that. She already lights up like a jar full of lightning bugs when she sees you. So does Colby. Be good for both of them if you stuck around." He grinned. "I don't know where Colby pulled your name from, but it seems to fit like a broken-in glove."

Before Faith could formulate a reply, Jack started taking things off the shelf and dropped them into the cart.

Wordlessly, she watched him select a big box of screws, spool of rope, four small cans, two blue and two green, a bucket of nails, and an assortment of hand tools, plus numerous small items she was clueless about. With each addition, he crossed it off on his list with a stubby pencil he also had in his jeans pocket.

"What are you going to do with all this?" she finally asked him.

Jack looked surprised, his hand resting on a shelf of bolts and rings of all sizes. "The Tica is a working ranch, ma'am. We always need stuff like this on a ranch." He motioned to the items he'd selected. "Things are always breaking or wearing out. Or Colby gets some bright idea, and we need supplies to bring it to a reality."

He pointed to a bucket of nails. "This allows us to repair loose shingles after a windstorm and to fix weak boards or a stall door." He picked up the rope. "This will lasso a steer or cow. Chain lets us pull a stuck calf or drag something behind the tractor. Lubricants and sprays are endless from easing a lock to cleaning our boots to fixing a squeaky door. And we always need duct tape around the place for half a dozen uses a day." He pointed to the four rolls of silver tape in the cart. "Hose clamps do just that, clamp a hose when it's spewing some liquid sky high. Hammers, screwdrivers, and other hand tools are always getting themselves lost or broken. And fencing is always needing attention whether it be barbed wire for the cattle, corrals for the horses or chicken wire for our breakfast makers."

"I had no idea."

Jack smiled. "That's okay, we'll turn you into a right proper ranching gal in no time. Now, we're done here. Let's go pay for all this and then I'll buy you a pie and coffee at Dimples."

Faith watched as the clerk tallied up their order. He and Jack made small talk about the weather, the size of heifers lately, the high price of hay, and a host of other topics, none of which Faith felt comfortable chiming in on. Finished, the clerk helped Jack carry the bags and buckets out to the truck. Faith carried two bags as well. They deposited all the supplies in the back of the truck, and Jack slammed the tail-gate up with a breathless smile.

"Thanks for the hand, friend." He shook hands with the clerk. Once the man turned to leave, Jack looked at Faith over the tailgate. "Faith, how about that pie and coffee now?"

She was about to agree when a sign caught her eye. "Can we make one more stop first?

"The library? You itching to read some books?" Jack scrubbed his chin.

Faith grinned at his perplexed expression. "Just cookbooks. I'd like to see if they have any cookbooks that don't feature beef and potatoes. Maybe some pasta dishes, or chicken, or vegetarian."

"There's nothing wrong with eating beef and potatoes, but I suppose pasta or chicken might be nice for a change." He wagged a finger in her direction. "But don't go getting any ideas of making us vegetarian meals. Colby and I will draw the line at that."

Faith giggled. "I suppose. Now, I promise to be quick."

"Ma'am, take your time. We've got plenty of it. I learned a long time ago to never rush a cow or mare delivering a baby or a woman on an errand."

Faith asked at the desk where to find cookbooks and trailed her fingertips over the titles. So many sizes? Big books, little books, fat books, thin books. She pulled them from the shelves, thumbed through the index and pictures of recipes. She murmured to herself as she read ingredients and cooking directions. She set some aside to sign out or placed most back on the shelf if they didn't appeal to her. Cooking for a group was not an easy task, and she was glad she only cooked for Colby, Sierra, and Jack. The crew had their own cook.

True to his word, Jack patiently waited, not once pushing her to hurry. He teased and flirted with the librarian for a while, until evidently, he grew bored, and he found a chair not far from the row Faith was in. He reclined back, watching her and anyone else walking around them. He reminded Faith of a furry guard dog from one of Sierra's storybooks.

Finally, she picked up her three choices and headed toward Jack. He rose to meet her. Suddenly she froze. "Jack,

I just realized, I don't have a library card. Don't I need one to check books out?"

"No need to fret, ma'am. Hand 'em over, and I can check 'em out under my card."

He once more flirted with the librarian while she scanned the titles.

"Doing some cooking, Jack?"

He stretched lazily. "Never hurts a man to grow his interests. Leastways until a woman comes along who can do it better."

The librarian rolled her eyes and glanced at Faith. "He's something, isn't he?" She slid the books into a bag proclaiming Crazy Woman Public Library and handed them to Faith. "Good luck, honey."

Jack feigned hurt, but tipped his hat to the librarian as he escorted Faith outside. "Now, how about that trip to Dimples, ma'am?"

"Absolutely."

They drove the short distance to Dimples and found an empty booth. Faith studied the menu and sighed.

"Tough choice, gal?"

She shook her head. "No. One of the many problems with amnesia is I don't remember or have any insight into what flavors I like. The pumpkin Colby and I shared the night of the dance was okay, but not great. And nothing here seems… I don't know…right."

Jack gave her a sympathetic gaze. "I could not imagine what it's like for you. Going to my comfort foods has kept me sane over the years. To not know what those were—" He gave up with a shake of his head. "Colby's the insightful one who could figure out what you might like. Or he'd make an optimistic guess." He cracked a grin. "I'd suggest just dropping your finger on one of the names and hoping it's palatable."

She nodded, closed her eyes, and dropped her finger. "Well, coconut cream it is. Here is hoping I like coconut."

"Either way, it's one more thing you can say you'll know about yourself by the time we leave here."

"That sounds like something Colby might say."

They shared a laugh as the server came for their orders.

"What can I get yous?"

"Two coffees, one coconut cream pie, and one Dutch apple."

The server, her name tag read Mona, scribbled it all on her notepad. "Sure thing, honey." She studied Faith, and then slid a long, hooded look to Jack. "I see you found someone new, Jack." She drew her lips into a pout.

Faith stiffened, but instinctively knew Mona was no threat. She sensed she normally experienced few threats and again wondered who or what kind of woman she was that jealous women, or even those pretending to be envious, were no threat to her.

Jack slapped the table with his hand. "Since you wouldn't give me the time of day anymore, Mona, I had to find me someone else."

Mona dipped her hip and stuck her pencil behind her ear. "I didn't see you at the festival dance. I might have let you take me for a spin or two around the floor."

"Nope. I had the pleasure of staying in with the sweetest little gal in all of Crazy Woman. Lil Sierra."

Mona's face softened. "That's for sure. That child certainly takes after her daddy. Ain't nothing like her mama. Lucy always was prone to wandering, whether with her feet, her eyes, or her hands. Hopefully, all that sweet baby gets from her mama is her beauty. I always felt Colby deserved better than Lucy." She touched Jack's hand and gazed over at Faith. "I'll be right back with your pies and coffees."

Faith leaned back in her seat and let out a breath. "She won't put anything in my food, will she?"

"No, course not. Mona just likes to play the victim sometimes; she means no harm. She enjoys the flirting."

So did Jack. She considered the conversation about Colby. It was interesting, and insightful, and frankly, quite personal. She already knew there were a few secrets and lots of opinions with the people around here. Again, it was unquestionably a culture she was not accustomed to, but it seemed the accepted normal. However, the unexpected benefit was it gave her more inside information about Colby. His wife was unhappy, and prone to roam, and their daughter took more after him than the mother who left them.

Both were optimistic, gregarious, insightful, inquisitive, and compassionate. She could already see the traits emerging from the seven-year-old.

Mona arrived with their coffee and dessert. She lingered an extra moment over placing Jack's cup and plate at just the perfect position. Faith watched, grinning at the spectacle. Jack flushed, which amused Faith even more.

"Well, do you like the coconut?" Jack asked a few moments later.

Faith took an extra bite, chewing thoughtfully. "It's all right, but clearly not something I would order as a rule. Not bad, just not a favorite."

Jack forked up a bite of his Dutch apple and held it out. "Here, try a bite and see if this is more to your liking."

Faith felt her eyes widen at the offer, then shrugged. "Okay." She took the fork, bit, and sampled the fare. She handed the fork back. "Yes, this is more what I think I like. Perhaps I'll stick to the fruit pies instead of cream ones."

Jack motioned Mona over. "How about another apple or fruit pie, please?"

Faith was about to protest when Jack interrupted her. "I'll eat the coconut; you can have something you like. How about cherry?"

Mutely she nodded, sure her neck was turning blush red. Mona promised to be right back.

"Faith, ma'am, I don't claim to know anything about you, but I'm not blind or dumb either. A woman ought to be treated like a prized mare, or fine treasure. But I got a feeling you don't know that, or maybe haven't experienced it. I don't know. So let me and Colby spoil you a little bit. It's good for you and makes us feel good too."

Jack's speech might not have been the most eloquent one she ever heard, but there was no mistaking the passion in his tone and his eyes. She reached across the table and gripped his hand. "Jack Jennings, you are a good man."

He laughed, smiling broadly. "Why sure I am. You catch on quick. I've been trying to tell Colby that for years." Then he reached for the coconut pie just as Mona returned with a slab of red cherry.

"I added a scoop of ice cream and whipped topping," she pointed out. "If you don't like it, Jack there sure will."

"Thank you, Mona, that was very kind." Once Mona smiled and walked away, Faith turned back to Jack. "I don't know if I like ice cream."

"Only one way to find out."

As Faith ate her dessert, and learned she liked both cherries and vanilla ice cream, she had more questions for Jack.

"One thing I don't understand, you and Colby have such different personalities. How did your friendship develop so strong despite your rough beginning and opposite characteristics?"

"That's easy to explain. First, I moved from Hidalgo County when I was six. After our first day at the principal's office, folks would say Colby and I were like two long-legged colts. Except he was seen as the promising Thoroughbred, and I was compared to the rowdy mustang." He stopped to push the coconut pie plate away and resume the apple slice. "But we had some great experiences. Oh my, the things we didn't think of. Especially as we got older."

Faith grinned and took the last bite of her dessert. "Are you sure it wasn't more the things you thought of and took Colby along?"

"There might have been a little of that too, I reckon, if I'm honest. Colby's the empathetic guy. Sensitive. He's a thinker. He's optimistic, always believing the best."

"And you?" Faith was fully caught up in Jack's words. She tried to see the two men as young boys or teenagers. It was difficult, but then again, it wasn't.

"I'm all of that stuff too. Just not in the same measurements as Colby. But that lil Sierra is working on me."

Faith smiled fondly. She was falling for that child. "Yes, she seems really good at bringing the best out of people."

"She never got that from her mama." Jack scoffed. "That's all her daddy's genes."

"It certainly sounds like that is the general opinion. You said you had been married before. Do you have any little ones of your own somewhere?"

Jack shook his head. "Nope, never had my own young 'uns. At least none that I know of. My first marriage lasted less than a year. We were too young to be married but didn't figure that out until afterwards. The second marriage lasted just a tad longer. Again, we had no clue how to be a husband and wife. Then, while I was drifting, riding, and trying to decide if I wanted to stay here in Henderson or go back to Hidalgo or tumble to wherever the wind might blow me, Colby bought The Tica and needed a foreman. Naturally, he turned to me right away."

"Naturally." She arched a dark brow.

"Colby is a special breed, ma'am, so don't misjudge him. He can be tough, and he can be tender. You should have been around when his horse died when we were kids. I thought he'd never quit bawling." Jack shook his head. "But he can also stand tall and face the wind when someone prods him. Or if he sees someone else being pushed around. He won't stand for it."

He sounds like the perfect man. The thought popped into Faith's mind. It was clear Jack thought much of his friend. Faith didn't know if she was the type to read romance books, but it seemed Colby was the essence of who might be the story's hero.

Her mind flashed back to that afternoon in front of the mirror, where he guessed her ethnicity as probably Italian. He noticed the smallest details about her face. His touch was so tender, despite his calloused hands. His gaze was soft and honest. He smelled like—

"Faith?"

She startled at the sound of her name. She inhaled and blinked. "I'm sorry, you were saying?"

"Any more coffee?" Mona asked, her tone impatient.

Jack just smiled over the rim of his cup, amused. Heat moved up Faith's neck. "No, no, I'm good, thank you." She peeked in her cup. There were still a few swallows left if she wanted them. What did Jack find so amusing? Unless he could somehow read her mind. Mona gave another irritated huff and swaggered away.

The diner's bell jingled over the front door, and two uniformed police officers walked in. Faith's gaze immediately swung to them and stayed on them until they took a seat a few booths away. She turned to Jack. "Well, isn't it about time we get moving on your list? This dessert was delicious." She started to get up before Jack could finish laying down the money.

Jack gave her a puzzled look but escorted her out the door.

CHAPTER **NINE**

Faith reached into the basket for another damp shirt and shook it out. Her eyes widened. Where has this been? Hiding out in the washing machine? Why'd it get put in the washing machine in the first place? It was the blouse she'd worn the first day she came to Tica. She studied it now, held up to eye level as she turned away from the sun's glare. The left sleeve was ripped. Two buttons were gone. Several small tears laced the shoulders. It looked like she wore it during a fight with a bear, and she lost. The bloody patches now faded to dull pink stains.

"It's trash now." Sighing, she wadded the blouse up and tossed it to the corner of the basket to throw away once she went inside. She retrieved another shirt and shook it out. Smaller, made of bright stripes and colors. She smiled at Sierra's sweatshirt. The child wore clothing as colorful as her personality.

This was the shirt Sierra had worn when they put up the decorations. It has been such fun and the men seemed so awed by their hard work. Faith meant what she told Jack;

Sierra was working herself into her heart. It was amazing and it was scary at the same time. Just like her daddy. Colby was a wonderful man with so many great characteristics, and Faith felt good, and safe, and appreciated when they were together. Qualities that felt foreign and she suspected were new. If Faith were not careful, between sweet Sierra and caring Colby, she may never want to find out about her old life. Like slipping into a warm bubble bath, she could simply slide into a new, permanent life here. If only the teasing bits of memories would leave her alone.

She was about to hang Sierra's sweatshirt over the line when the rumble of an engine made her pause. Dust rose along the driveway. Colby? No, this vehicle was green. Wrong color, so this was a visitor. How was she expected to welcome a guest here? She tried to recall how she might have received visitors before, in her previous life, and came up blank. She gave up with a heavy sigh of disappointment and watched a stout woman step from the green pickup.

"Faith, right? I'm Margie. We met at the dance."

Of course. Along with the rest of the county's population. The woman did look familiar. Faith nodded. "Yes, welcome to Tica."

"Thanks. I've come to buy some eggs. Do you have a couple extra dozen?"

Colby sold eggs? She pictured Sierra and her chore every morning to collect eggs. Sometimes Faith tagged along, although frankly, she found the entire process of eggs from bird to skillet rather nauseating, and she considered the henhouse revolting. "Er…Colby isn't here now."

Margie waved her words away. "That's fine. You can take my money as easily as he can." She laughed as if it were some inside joke. "My mother-in-law is coming, and I need the eggs for baking. Colby's hens lay the best eggs around."

"Alright," Faith agreed slowly and headed for the kitchen. "But aren't all eggs the same?" She didn't want to cost Colby a sale, but Margie seemed determined to get his eggs, and only his.

"No, no, dear. It depends on the health and breed of hen, and the bird's diet and age. Those all combine to create a good egg. Colby does something to his hens to make them so perfect."

The man could charm his chickens like he charmed her? They reached the kitchen and Faith removed two cardboard cartons from their supply under the counter. She still felt they needed to be in the refrigerator, but Colby assured her that wasn't the case with fresh eggs. Margie didn't seem bothered by the carton's location either.

"Here ya go, honey. Thank you." She pushed a twenty-dollar bill into Faith's hand.

That seemed excessive. "I can get you some change—" she began, remembering Colby kept a coffee can on top of the refrigerator for spare change and leftover bills.

"No, no. These here are worth it. Especially with the mother-in-law coming." She gave Faith a conspiratorial wink and waved goodbye. Faith reached above the fridge for the coffee can, dropped the twenty inside, and heard the rev of the engine as Margie left.

People here seemed so strange, but what did she really have to measure them against? She let out a sigh and returned to hanging the laundry.

❄

"Colby, buddy, I don't know much about this crazy life, but I do know one thing: your pretty little filly is running scared. Even if she doesn't remember what, sure as bulls like cows she's running from something. I'd bet my last dollar on that."

Colby exhaled a deep breath and kicked the bale of hay from the flatbed trailer to the ground where the bawling cattle eagerly tore into it. He shook his head and looked over at Jack. "You'd better keep that dollar. You saw those bruises all over her. I'm not surprised she's scared of something. Of someone." He sure wished he knew *who* scared her. He'd have a man to man talk with that person and educate him on how a man is supposed to properly treat a lady. He scrubbed his jaw and then maneuvered another bale into position and cut the strings.

"Honestly, Jack, think about it. Imagine being her, bruised and battered, clothing torn and bloody, but not having a memory of what happened and who did it to you. Now she's out here with you, me, and the other ranch hands drifting around. You know you'd be scared of your shadow if that was you. I'd be jumpy as a cricket in the chicken coop."

"She was fine while we were hitting the stores and first at Dimples. She only got nervous after the police came in."

Colby shook his head. That made no sense. She'd been fine at the police station when they went. Or had she? He kicked the bale out and watched it bounce along the ground. He lined up another bale, his thoughts going back. He'd been so worried the police would find a missing person report, and she'd have to go back. Maybe he had not noticed her nervousness because of his own fears. "I just don't know, Jack."

What did it matter if Faith was scared or running? He couldn't blame her for being afraid. The images of finding her in bare feet, her fine quality clothing torn, and bruises of various ages peppering her body never left him alone for long. Even without the ringless finger, those facts alone proved there was someone in her past she deemed worth escaping.

He winced, thinking of her bruises. Just this morning he studied them, hoping he wasn't being obvious. Some were fading to an angry yellow centered, red ring, and surrounded by dark blue rings. They reminded him of bullseyes. And he'd love to plow his fists into the jack-wad who put them on her, as if the creep painted bullseyes on his face. Other, older bruises shrank to small navy-blue spots, just about ready to fade completely away. If only his anger faded so easily. And the freshest marks were still puffy, and black and blue, aggravated and doubtlessly tender. Sometimes he'd catch Faith gently rubbing one or two welts, and he fought to keep from going to her and try kissing the pain away. It worked with Sierra when she had a boo-boo, but while he doubted it worked the same with Faith, he sure wanted to try.

He exhaled deeply and shook his head and kicked another bale of hay out to the mooing cows. Until her memories returned, he doubted she'd run, since she had nowhere to go. It sounded terrible, and he dared not say the words out loud, but he was relieved she was more or less stranded at the ranch. Did that make him a horrible person?

If she were just skittish when the police were around, it made no sense to him, but he felt it made some sense to Faith, whether she was guided by memories or just a gut feeling. He'd prefer she open up and talk to him about her concerns. He might not be able to do much, but he could listen to her. He could support her emotionally.

Jack yanked a hay bale over, cut the twine, and booted it over the edge. Cows attacked it before it bounced once and landed. "I do know this much; these critters are hungry." He banged his fist on the top of the cab to let the driver up front know to move forward to the next drop off point.

Faith swung the sheet over the line and clipped it with the wooden pins. She brushed her hair out of her eyes with the back of her hand. Laundry was a never-ending chore. It boggled her mind how just the three of them could generate so much stuff to wash!

However, she had to agree with Sierra and Colby that sheets and blankets dried out in the cool Texas sunshine smelled so nice when she fell into bed at night. Colby had already assured her by summer all the laundry would be hung in the warm sunshine. Right now, she brushed the light sprinkle of snow aside with her foot. What tiny bit of snow that still lingered would be melted before midday.

It was unbelievable how much hard work it was to run a ranch! She truly did fall into bed at night. She took turns cooking breakfast, and felt proud that she mastered scrambled eggs, frying ham, bacon or sausage, and she could adequately mix and cook pancakes or fry diced potatoes and squeeze oranges for fresh-squeezed juice. Sierra was a patient teacher. And Faith could whip up sandwiches and canned soups for lunch and was happy to observe Colby or Jack as they made a mouth-watering dinner.

While the men tackled farm chores, she washed the

dishes, washed the laundry, swept the floors, changed linens, sometimes collected chicken eggs, and found countless other small things to help. Maybe not so small to her, but Colby assured her they made life a bit easier on the others. She assisted Sierra with her homework until she was out of school for Christmas break. She had to agree ranching was hard work.

She just finished securing the last bedsheet to the line when she heard the clip clop of horse hooves.

"Faith!"

Sierra's shout drew her attention over to the barn. Colby and Sierra walked toward her, leading three horses. She recognized Sierra's pony, Topper, and Colby's horse he called Ben.

"Wanna go for a ride with us, Faith?" Sierra asked excitedly.

Panic struck her. "I…I, umm, don't…" She stumbled over an excuse.

Sierra turned her head sideways, like a pleading puppy. "It's the first day of school break. You gotta go riding with us."

She looked into Sierra's hopeful eyes and then forced herself to look at Colby. Big mistake.

"Faith, I reckon riding isn't a favorite thing of yours, but that doesn't mean it can't become one." Colby's rich, timbered, voice reached out to her like velvet. He extended his hand, the leather reins of the other horse looping over his palm. "Come ride with us. Please."

Her knees trembled, and it had nothing to do with fear of the horse or riding up so high. It had everything to do with his silky voice, hooded eyes, and seductive charm. She knew, memories or not, that no man had ever made her feel so weak-kneed before. And he was simply asking her to go for a horse ride with him and his daughter. What if he were to ask her for something cozier?

"I…" She stepped toward Colby, her eyes hooked on his tender gaze, her hand reaching automatically for his extended palm. She touched his hand, the rawhide reins between them cool to the touch.

He curled his fingers over hers as if afraid she might pull away. His Adam's apple bobbed once. "This is Matilda. She's a gentle ride."

His soft words, whispered in his rough-edged tone washed over her. She could listen to that velvety rumble all day. Before she could reconsider, he guided her to the brown horse. She looked the creature in the eye, studying the long face, the white stripe down its nose was a sharp contrast to the reddish-brown fur, the gentle deep brown eyes, and chocolate whiskers on its grey-brown muzzle. Its breath was moist and warm. She breathed out a heavy sigh. "Matilda. I hope you plan to take it easy on me."

Colby chuckled behind her. His hands came to her waist and flashbacks of their moments on the dance floor rushed over her.

"Matilda only knows how to be easy. She will be perfect for you." Colby moved one hand to her left hand on the front of the saddle and her right hand on the back. Then his hand dipped to her left leg. "You put your left foot in the stirrup. I'll do the rest."

She obeyed, half afraid to move beyond that. Her breath lodged in her chest. The leather was cool under her hands but stretching her leg up to the stirrup-y thing felt unnatural. Colby's hands returned to her waist, and she sucked in a breath, cold over her teeth. Her next thought was of moving up and through the air. He raised her upwards, and she feared he was throwing her over the back of the horse. Air rushed out of her mouth in a surprised yelp. Before she could catapult to the other side, he guided her to a sitting position. Leather squeaked as she settled into the saddle's deep groove.

Still anchored by his hands, she looked at him in amazement. He seemed unaware of her shock.

He rested one hand on her knee. "You did good. Now keep this foot in this stirrup and hook your right foot into the right one. But only stick your toes in the iron, not your whole foot. Point your toes out by slightly bending your knees. Keep your back straight and aligned with your hips. Sit deep into the saddle."

She'd never dream it was so complicated to sit. But Colby wasn't done.

"You hold the reins with your fingers, and your palm turned up. Never wrap the leather around your fingers or wrist. Keep your elbows bent at a ninety-degree angle and aligned with your hips. Think straight from head, neck, through your spine and hips. Keep a light but firm grip on your reins. Matilda has a soft mouth, so it won't take much pressure to guide her. Okay, you got it?"

She nodded, not sure what to think. She sure didn't get any of this. Soft mouth? Guide Matilda? Ninety degrees? Think straight? Light but firm? *What?* She wanted his hands back on her knee and wrapped around her hand. She wanted him to look at her with that tender gaze. She wanted his rich, silky, rumbling voice talking to her, no matter what he was saying. He could explain horse terms she didn't understand or read Shakespeare. As long as his voice rumbled near her and his gaze stayed on her, she didn't care what he said.

Yet she nodded, aware Sierra was waiting patiently. The horse, Matilda, stomped its front foot as Colby moved away and she panicked.

"Oh! Wait! What's it doing? What's that mean?" She had no clue how to speak horse. Visions of the horse leaping away, dropping her into the dirt like a ragdoll flooded her mind.

Colby laughed. "Easy, Faith. Horses do that. It can mean absolutely nothing, or they're bored, or maybe a fly is bugging them, or it can mean hurry up. In this case, I'd warrant Matilda wants to get going."

Sure it did. Whatever. She'd take his word for it. She watched as both Sierra and Colby swung into their saddles with a practiced, familiar, and easy grace. She appreciated the rugged picture Colby made, making her heart flutter like a bunch of butterflies.

Sierra took the lead, urging her pony ahead. "Follow me. I know a good place to ride."

"Wait! How do I make it go?"

Colby rode Ben alongside her and reached for her hands. "Light touch. You give the reins the gentlest jiggle and tell her to move forward."

"That's all?"

Again, Colby chuckled. "Well, you can also cluck. Like this?" He moved his tongue against the roof of his mouth and fabricated a clicking sound that she had no hope of reproducing. It sounded similar to the barnyard chickens clucking. Between whatever combination, Matilda the horse moved ahead, falling into step behind Sierra and Topper. Colby brought up the end of the line.

Sierra rode like a professional. Faith had seen her riding Topper before, but now that she was part of the group, she quickly developed a new appreciation of what went into riding. Sierra's experience and enthusiasm showed through as she trotted her pony along familiar trails. The girl was a natural and clearly in her element. Faith was acutely aware of Colby following on his larger horse. She focused on his directions, staying straight, keeping a light touch, and all those vague instructions, and thought only of wanting to look back at him. Would that make Matilda turn around?

She found Matilda's rhythm and thanked her lucky stars it was smooth and steady. Here she breathed heavier than standing around the ranch and the brisk air felt surprisingly good on her face and rushing through her lungs. They left the barns and skirted the fields. Faith looked at the cattle looking back at them. They flicked their long ears and swished their tails. She easily identified the ones Colby called Longhorns and assumed the smaller reddish-brown ones were the Herefords. They bawled and mooed, sounding forlorn.

In a way, she sympathized with them. She had several moments in which she just gave up and cried, though probably for a different reason than these cows.

The horses snorted. The smell of pine and horse permeated the air. Sierra's happy chatter filtered back to Faith, meeting Colby's answering laugh. The saddle leather creaked as she followed Matilda's rocking movements. The rawhide reins warmed in her palms. Overhead, birds startled from the tree boughs. The flapping of their wings sounded so loud compared to the relative quiet around them. Faith felt as though they had been transported to a magic place, far away from any other people. Just the three of them.

They stopped beside a small pond, and Faith looked at their reflections, lined up at the water's edge. Colby sat tall and proud on his big horse. Sierra sat equally proud next to him. And she sat on Colby's other side, her reflection in the water, looking like she knew what she was doing. She smiled at her reflection, as if sharing a secret. Only she knew how nervous she'd been when they started out, how her knees trembled for the first several minutes. Now, she wished their ride would never end.

The reflections moved, and she glanced over at Colby. He caught her eye and sent her a flirty wink. Yes, she'd be happy to just keep riding with these two.

CHAPTER **TEN**

"I'm glad you and Sierra insisted I go on that ride. I had a wonderful time." Faith said. Colby sat next to her on the sofa. Sierra had gone to bed and together they cuddled and watched the Christmas lights on the tree blink, casting twinkles of gold and silver, red and green throughout the room. The fire crackled as its flames reached up the chimney. Evergreen and cinnamon filled the room, and leftover popcorn. Carols played on the radio. George Strait sang "Merry Christmas Wherever You Are". Jeff Carson had just finished singing about how Santa got lost in Texas.

Colby's arm rested over Faith's neck, warming her skin. His fingers traced lazy circles on her shoulder. She felt lulled into a state of utter relaxation. His voice rumbled near her ear.

He kissed the top of her head. "You're most welcome. And you and Sierra did a great job decorating here. I can really feel the Christmas spirit." He paused. "Even if you didn't hang any mistletoe."

"Jack promised to get some. He said the Plaza was out and he needed to go into town."

He scoffed and she knew her teasing hit its mark. The jealous moment was over in a flash, and Colby returned to the conversation at hand.

"I'm glad you enjoyed your time with us. You are welcome to go riding with me anytime. Sierra never stopped talking about it the entire time I put her to bed."

"Here, I thought you were reading her a story."

His chuckle vibrated against her shoulder. "Nope. She was telling me all about the ride, as if I hadn't been there. But to be fair, I wasn't watching the birds, or critters or any stuff she talked about. I was watching you."

Faith feigned surprise. "And I assumed you rode in the back to keep an eye out for danger and protect us." She gently smacked his thigh.

"Oh, I would have protected you two, with my life if necessary. But it's a well-known fact that riding in the rear usually gives the best views."

Faith slapped his thigh again. He laughed and captured her hand in his. She turned to look up at him. His smile shined as bright as the lights on the tree. His eyes danced merrily like the flames in the fireplace. She felt his mirth against her shoulder and smiled in reply. He dropped his head and rested his forehead against her shoulder, his hair tickling her neck. He sighed deeply.

"Colby?"

"Just thinking about tomorrow. I don't look forward to going to court. Seeing my ex-in-laws after all this time. Things didn't end well when Lucy left. And fighting for the right to have my daughter is just stupid."

She patted his thigh, this time in sympathy. "It does seem

idiotic. I can't help but wonder if they have an ulterior motive."

"You mean some reason other than just wanting to rip Sierra away from me?"

She winced at the anger, frustration, and hurt in his voice. Did his ex-in-laws have any idea how much it would kill him if they were successful and took his child away? Would they care if they knew his deep love for the girl? She swallowed, bringing her mind back to the question. "Yes. Do you think she could unwittingly serve some other purpose for them?"

He pulled back and looked at her, his expression a mix of somberness and astonishment. "Nothing I can think of. What could a seven-year-old child bring to grandparents who haven't been a part of her life since she's been out of diapers? Honestly, Faith, sometimes the things you say make me wonder about your past."

She nodded solemnly, wondering herself where the thought had come from. It wasn't the first time she'd mentioned something no one else had considered, something outside the box of normal expectations. "Me too, Colby. Me too."

He pecked her cheek. "I reckon they just got some bee in their bonnet, thinking they can be better parents for Sierra because they're a two-parent family. A mommy and daddy or granny and gramps in this case. And they have boatloads of money."

Faith wondered what the in-laws' relationship with their daughter was lately but knew Colby would have no way of knowing. Both he and Jack, and most of the town, made it clear she had not been heard or seen since the day she left. Is that where Sierra might fit in?

She stroked his knee. "Yes, children should have both a mom and a dad. But you know, Colby, we can also make a good two-parent family for her. Together we are a mommy and a daddy too." Something stirred in her memory, slipping away before she could capture it. Was it because she was already a mom? Or was it a memory of her mom? She gave up with a sigh and rubbed his leg again.

Colby sniffed, and she wondered if he'd been silently crying. He drew back to look at her and she noticed the moisture in his eyes. His vulnerability touched her. A man weeping over his daughter. Had her father ever shed a tear over her? She'd like to know.

"There's nothing I'd like more, Faith. But I'm not sure if I should tell the judge or not."

"But if it helps your case—"

He placed a finger against her lips. Warmth touched the soft skin around her mouth. "Of course, it would help, but what if you discover your past life and return to it?"

A partial phrase surfaced in her mind. *What the law doesn't know, doesn't hurt me.* Where did that come from? What did it mean? Whatever it was, a chill slipped over her.

Colby stood outside his truck, hand on the door. He closed his eyes, sucked in a deep breath, and thought of Faith. Her smile just before he left the house was the only thing to get him through this meeting. She'd cupped his jaw, smiled sweetly, and he inhaled the syrup and cinnamon on her breath from their French toast breakfast. He considered kissing her. Sierra was off gathering eggs by the barn, and they were alone, and he was hard-pressed to think of a reason not to touch her lips.

"Colby, you are the best person to raise Sierra. You and I can be the two-parent team that she needs. Go to that meeting and prove to your ex-in-laws that they seriously misjudged you. Capire fischi per fiaschi."

He froze at the unfamiliar phrase. "What does that mean?"

She blinked, as if startled by her words. "I... I...think it means they're barking up the wrong tree."

"You know Italian?" He was glad she was getting more memories back, but it also scared him half to death.

"Evidently so." She licked her lips. He knew a subconscious memory had just surfaced, whether she understood it or not. She knew the words, and what they meant, even if she didn't remember anything else. This was happening more and more. He took her hands in his and kissed her lips, after all. Then he thanked her, grabbed his hat, and headed out the door. And now here he was, about to go talk to the judge.

This was the informal discussion, just him, them, and the judge. No lawyers. They each had a chance to explain to the judge why they were the better ones to raise Sierra. If they could not work this out amicably, which he doubted they could, or if the judge could not decide, it was time to bring in the lawyers and hash it out in an official, and costly, trial. So he would take Faith's advice, present them as a unified front of two people, ready to raise Sierra as a couple. They stood a better chance of swaying the judge than just him alone as a single father. And if they were successful and she ended up someday leaving them, which he hoped did not happen, at least he would still have Sierra.

He whispered a prayer and headed into the courthouse, looking for room 71A. He found the office, checked in and was escorted to an inner room. Lucy's parents sat by the paneled wood door. Lucy's mom dressed impeccably in a pencil skirt, blouse and coordinating blazer and heels. Her dad wore pressed slacks and crisp polo shirt. Colby felt like a bumpkin in his jeans and work shirt, but he gave them a nod. Lucy's dad returned with a brief nod of his own. Her mother narrowed her bright red lips and lifted her chin so high she'd drown if she was caught in a rainstorm. As if she read his thoughts, she turned her head the other way. Maybe she just did it because she didn't like looking at him. Well, no love lost between them.

Colby made himself comfortable as far as he could from them, considering it was a small waiting room. Tension mounted with each passing minute, as palatable as the stench of an irritated skunk. He set his jaw, pictured Sierra's big, happy smile and resolved he'd succeed at this. For his daughter.

Thankfully, they were soon called into the judge's chambers, and thankfully a larger space. He took a chair on one side of the U-shaped table; Lucy's parents took chairs on the other side, and the judge and his assistant sat in the middle. Peacekeepers? Or agents of justice?

Leah—or Lucy's mother, as he preferred to remember his former mother-in-law—was quick to take the lead in the discussion. She planted her palms on the table and fixed the judge with a concerned stare.

"Your Honor, this man is inadequate to raise my granddaughter, and his place is unfit to keep her safe." She stabbed a finger across at Colby.

This man? She couldn't even address him by name? He

tamped down his emotions, remembering Jack's parting advice last night that she would try to get him worked up and make him look unstable. He had to remain in control of his emotions.

The judge looked over at him for a rebuttal. "Your Honor, Sir, I've not only kept my daughter safe and thriving since their daughter—my former wife—left nearly seven years ago, but I've built a solid reputation in town as a good father and positive role model. I have letters here from my pastor at church, a deacon there and two business owners in town, all vouching for my character. I also have a letter from Sierra's teacher in school and one from her Sunday school teacher. There is also my most recent financial statement as well." He handed the packet of documents over, feeling as though they were sheets of gold.

The judge shuffled the papers, glancing over them, then he looked over at Leah and Daryll.

Leah harrumphed. "Your Honor. So he has some letters. So what?" She waved her hand dismissively. "We also have letters from some business acquaintances and members of our country club. However, letters prove little. The fact remains, it is impossible for him to adequately provide for a young, vulnerable girl. It is just him and some men on a ranch in the middle of nowhere. That is hardly a fitting place to raise a little girl."

Funny how Lucy didn't mind living on a ranch in the middle of nowhere. Until she decided she did. Colby shook the thought aside. Leah must have determined his moment to think as meaning he had no reply, so she plowed ahead again.

"All he has is a cow farm. He has no availability to

provide for a child. We, on the other hand, can offer her a city with culture, refinement, arts, and a quality education."

"Crazy Woman might not have all the refinement and congestion of Dallas." Darn, he meant to say cosmopolitan and instead inserted his opinion of Dallas' overcrowding. Apparently, Leah didn't notice.

"Exactly. He is depriving my granddaughter of the right to expand her horizons and grow in knowledge."

"As I was about to say, Your Honor, Sir, we don't have everything Dallas has, but we have things here you won't find there."

"Such as, Mr. Lonigan?"

"Small town values. Respect. Integrity. Honest work ethics. Pride in our history. A place where neighbors watch out for each other, and kids can play without worrying about constant dangers. Folks might be a mite nosy, but they all care for one another. Sierra has her friends here. We just put up the Christmas decorations, and she has had so much fun stringing lights and turning the living room into a winter wonderland. We went to the local Christmas fair recently and she saw Santa and gave him her list. She is learning the real meaning of Christmas and what it means to show the true spirit."

The judge raised his hand. "I get the picture you are painting. Thank you."

"Your Honor, he thinks a few holiday baubles and a local backwards fair can compare to what we can do for her? We can take her to Europe for the holidays, not a country fair. We can provide anything she wants or needs year-round, not just in December after she sits on a fat man's lap with a wish list. We can offer her so much more. He can only offer her a small town, hard work, history, and nosy people. We can offer her two people to live with and raise her to appreciate the finer things. Dallas is renowned for—"

"Ma'am, I am well versed in what Dallas is renowned for. I am from Dallas myself."

Colby's heart sank. In the whole state of Texas, their judge had to hail from the same city Leah and Daryll lived? He swallowed, wishing for water. "Your Honor, Sir. I can offer Sierra two people as well."

"You and a bunch of dirty ranch hands hardly count." Leah cut in. "What will my granddaughter learn? To chew and spit tobacco, drink, and smoke, and shoot a gun?"

"Your honor, Sir, I hold a graduate Bachelor of Science from the University of Texas Austin. So does my foreman where he graduated with a bachelor in business. Most of my crew are college graduates in science, agriculture, and other fields, or they are currently working on their degrees. We all have advanced education. Most of us earned them from the University of Texas."

Colby paused for a breath. "A few of the crew smoke or chew, but drinking is forbidden on the ranch, and we only shoot guns when there's trouble."

The judge nodded and Leah huffed. "Your honor, they may have been to a college and made the correct motions. But the fact is, there is no female presence there to guide her. What will happen when she gets older and starts asking female questions? Where will she get her womanly advice from at a ranch full of men? You can bet their agricultural degrees did not prepare them for that."

Leah was getting on his nerves, just like Jack forecasted she would. He wondered if the judge felt he was watching a tennis match with all the back and forth between him and Leah.

"I have a female guest staying on the ranch. With me." There. It was said. He felt cornered, but Leah was playing dirty, and he needed to blurt the words out before he lost his will.

"You remarried?" Leah hissed as she slowly rose in her chair.

She reminded Colby of a rattlesnake, coiling up, tongue flickering, tail rattling, and ready to strike. He wondered what the difference was to her. It was her daughter who left and divorced him. It was no concern of hers if he wanted to remarry. Except it provided both a mom and dad for Sierra. "Not exactly." He glanced at the judge, who waited with raised eyebrows and crossed arms.

"We might marry. We've talked about it. But…er…first she needs to remember who she is." Colby winced. Oh, doggee, didn't that sound strange? The judge's brows now creased together in a frown like an upside-down V.

"Remember, Mr. Lonigan? Who is this female guest?"

"Well, Sir, Your Honor, we don't really know. When I found her, she was lost and had amnesia. We've been to the police and checked around, but no one seems to be missing her. Her fingerprints aren't in any of their databases either. So she's staying on at the ranch until her memories return."

"And you intend to marry this woman, Mr. Lonigan?"

Why did the way the judge say that make it sound crazy? Because it did… sort of. He nodded, not daring a look at Leah and Daryll. He didn't have to look; he could hear her reaction well enough. And feel it transmitting through the air like wavelengths of emotions.

She was less impressed than the judge was. Her fists hit the table. He glanced over and watched her stand straight up to her five-foot two-inch height.

"Your Honor, this cannot be real." She flung her hand at him like a witch about to cast a spell. "He has an unknown woman staying with him, who claims to have lost her memory. Even if that were true, she could be anyone. Or anything. She could be faking her so-called amnesia. This is reckless endangerment! She needs to be put in a hospital or somewhere, not left with my granddaughter!" She clutched her chest. "My word! What if that woman was alone with that dear, innocent child right now!"

Anger and regret warred within Colby. This was not going the way he'd hoped. He felt he was spending more time defending himself, and not explaining why he was the better parent. If Leah had her way, the judge wouldn't even see him as a decent human. And heaven only knew what he'd think about Faith. He glanced at the judge, noting the wrinkled brow and pursed lips. The guy probably listened to crazy families all day long, every day. He'd happily take on an ornery longhorn cow fighting over her calf any day than deal with this stuff.

Leah's drama was causing him a headache.

Colby finally left the courthouse, stood at the bottom of the steps, and exhaled deeply. He raked a hand through his sweat-dampened hair and plunked his cowboy hat back on.

Ahead of him walked Leah and Darryl. His stomach curled as he watched Leah's proud saunter. Once upon a time he thought Lucy carried herself in the same manner as her mother; except back then he stupidly called it sexy. He paused at his truck, rested a hand on the hood and watched them climb into a bright red, new model luxury car. While he might not recognize the emblem on the hood, and he sure couldn't afford to own one, he surely knew how to spot an overpriced frilly car.

Oh mercy, but he needed a break. While he was anxious to return to Faith and Tica, he also needed to compose himself before joining his loved ones.

First, he fished his phone out and called Faith explaining he'd be another hour, then he walked over to Dimples. The lunch crowd was long gone, and the dinner crowd had not started.

"Hey, Colby, coffee?" Mona called, looking up as he entered. He nodded and looked around.

A couple of ranch hands from the Square D sat around a table, looking over some paperwork. A business meeting of sorts. Three women laughed over dessert. He knew they were local wives. He tipped his hat. Stan Nickols, owner of the Narnia Ranch, sat with his cell phone, laptop, and coffee. Colby felt he needed to be alone, waved at Stan and took a seat at a back booth. He eyed the list of sandwich specials and decided he wasn't that hungry. Actually, the thought of food churned his stomach.

Mona, his server, brought the coffee and the morning newspaper. With the meeting so fresh—and sour—in his thoughts, Colby was grateful for the chance to think about something else. He sipped his coffee and idly flipped the pages and scanned the headlines. World, local, sports, and weather; not a lot to read. Two babies born at the hospital last month and old man Fletcher died at the ripe age of one hundred and two. It didn't take long, and he was caught up on all that was current.

He folded the paper and left it for the next patron as the front door swung open. Hal Campbell entered, his boots heavy on the old tile floor. Hal owned the Rocking C Ranch, bordering his on the other side of the Crazy Woman Creek. Hal stopped a few feet inside and spread his arms wide.

"Everyone, stay where you are. I'm buying the next round for everyone."

The cook looked over the counter and scowled at him. "Hal, you know we don't serve no alcohol here."

Hal pshawed. "Course I know that. I'm buying everyone a round of coffee. Fill 'er up, ladies!"

"You win the lottery, Hal?"

"Find a rich relative?"

"Even better. I struck gold." He dipped his hand into his pocket. "Look at this beauty."

Colby looked at the fluorescent lights glittering off a large diamond ring and his heart dropped to his toes and his stomach clawed up his throat with hot fingers. He leaned closer.

Stan whistled. "That's a pretty ring. Who you gonna give it to? I didn't know you were serious about someone."

Hal shook his head. "No, I found this beauty and next I'm gonna cash in on it. You can tell it's valuable."

Colby had no doubt it was valuable. And he had no doubts whatsoever it belonged to anyone but Faith. He itched to hold it for a moment. From his seat he could see the diamond was large, dazzling brilliantly under the lights, and set in a gold band.

"How can you tell if it's real or not?" Stan persisted.

Hal was not to be swayed by his friend. "It has '24K' stamped on the inside of the band, so that means it's twenty-four karat gold. That's worth a lot of money. And it won't stick to a magnet. And it scratched mama's ceramic plate, leaving a gold trace. Mama wasn't too happy about her plate."

Stan still frowned and reached for the ring. "And how do

you know the diamond is real? It could be zirconia just set in a fancy band."

"Nope. It's genuine too." Hal smiled big. "I dropped it in a glass of water, and it sank."

Stan scoffed. "Course it sank. It's a ring."

"Real diamonds sink and fakes float. And it wouldn't scratch a stone or a mirror. I tried both."

A few guys reached for their cell phones, quickly typing. Probably checking if that was true. Colby had to remind himself to breathe. Stan handed it back. "It's someone's ring. They'll be wanting it back. Looks like a woman's ring."

"You ought to take it to the police station."

"Are you kidding? I found it, out on the range, no one around for miles, so it's mine."

Stan harrumphed. "Hal, that's not the way that works, unless you're five years old."

Colby realized Hal and Stan would go on like this forever. They always could. He rose, steadying himself on the table before approaching Hal. "May I see?" he asked, fighting to keep his voice and expression neutral. Hal placed it in his palm, and he curled his fingers around the warm metal.

Breathe, Colby. Breathe.

He opened his eyes; not aware he even closed them. The ring was gorgeous. The diamond was as large as his pinky fingernail, flanked by three smaller diamonds on each side. It was meant to be noticed and admired. It cost some guy a good chunk of money to buy this. So why wasn't it on her finger? He attempted to size it by placing it over his left pinky. It made it to the first knuckle, and he stopped. Yes, this would fit Faith just about perfectly. And… it was an engagement ring only, not a wedding band.

"Won't fit you," Hal said. "It's meant for a lady."

Colby ignored him, instead looking carefully along the inside band. All he saw was the 24K, like Hal said was there. He swallowed, dread covering him like a blanket in summer. It felt like a metal brand someone had put on her finger, to show everyone he owned her. Like he owned his cattle and branded them to show everyone else they were his.

He exhaled. Despite the ring's beauty, value, and sparkle, it soured his stomach, turning the coffee to mud. Regretfully, he returned it to Hal. "Where'd you find it?"

Breathe, breathe…

"My north pasture, 'bout halfway between the fence and the woods. Why?"

Colby shook his head. Why was Faith's ring there? Had she thrown it while running from her fiancé? Hal's north pasture butted up to a big patch of woodlands and the Crazy Woman Creek. "Stan's right. It belongs to someone. Turn it in to the police."

Not that he was ever likely to take Faith to claim it. He hated the ring, but he felt he needed to side with someone, and Stan made the most sense. He usually did.

Before Hal could complain, or argue, Colby walked away. He handed Mona a five for his coffee and walked outside. There, supporting himself against the brick wall, he heaved a ragged breath. At least he now knew Faith was engaged, and not currently married. He started walking for his truck when a new possibility struck him cold, freezing him mid-stride.

Unless she dropped the wedding band too and Hal only found one, not both.

CHAPTER ELEVEN

Faith swept dried leaves and chunks of hay from the porch while Sierra read out loud to her and the rooster. She had to wonder just how common this was. She would almost bet where she was from—wherever she was from—this would be unheard of. However, the sight was so precious, she wondered how she lived so long without enjoying this. Automatically, her thoughts shifted to Colby.

He called a little bit ago, simply saying he was done at the courthouse, and planned to go over to Dimples for a few moments for coffee and to decompress before he came back. She'd wanted to ask how the meeting had gone or gauge something through his words, but he only sounded strained, and certainly in need of a short break. So she was resigned to waiting. Was he able to convince the judge to allow Sierra to stay? She could not imagine him having to give her up to strangers.

She listened to Sierra sounding out the tough words and smiled. This was a new book she hadn't heard before. It had penguins and tutus, princesses, and magical places. The last book she read was about a young girl and her talking cat who lived in a tree. She liked how Colby insisted she read paper books, not from an electronic device. She played with real toys, dolls, trucks, and stuffed animals, and no hand-held gaming pads.

There were only two computers on the ranch: one in Colby's office for business use and one in Jack's place for cattle records, reports, and employee files. He said he knew some of the crew had laptops and fancy phones, but he didn't care as long as they still worked when they should.

She noticed a cloud of dust in the distance. Colby? She turned back to the girl as she noticed a pause in her reading. "That's very good, honey. You read well."

Sierra nodded as she caressed the chicken. "Umm hmm. And this is a tough book too. Lots of hard words."

Faith smiled. "Yes, but you sounded them out like a pro."

"Faith? Can I say something?"

She set the broom aside, aware Sierra had closed her book. The girl's expression was serious, and Faith wondered what had her so intense. She sat down next to her, a safe distance from her pet rooster. "Of course, sweetie. What is it?"

Sierra's gaze studied her. "What's it like to not remember anything?"

She exhaled. That was not what she expected. She'd half thought this would involve another request for a horse ride. She clasped her hands in front of her and exhaled again. "Well, it's hard to explain. Have you ever forgotten something important?"

"I sometimes forget to bring my field day permission slips home to daddy."

Faith assumed that was as close to forgetting a seven-year-old might get. "All right. How did that make you feel?"

"Bad. Daddy has to call the school and talk to the principal then."

"Um…. Amnesia is a little different. I can still remember how to do things, and how stuff works, and how to walk and talk. What I've forgotten are the memories of my life. Who I knew, where I went to school, what I like to eat." And where she spent Christmas and who gave her the missing ring. "It's the personal details that I miss. Imagine one day you suddenly forget your Uncle Jack and your daddy. Imagine looking in the mirror and not recognizing your reflection. Imagine knowing you know how to ride, but don't remember ever riding Topper or that he's your pony. Imagine forgetting where you go to school, your teacher, and all your classmates and friends."

Tears welled in Sierra's eyes. "I can never forget daddy and Uncle Jack. They are my whole family."

Faith's heart stilled. What would she do if she were ripped away from her family and forced to live with her mother's parents? People she didn't even know. "But with amnesia, you don't get to decide what you remember and don't. It simply wipes every personal memory away like cleaning a chalkboard."

Sierra sniffed and scooted closer to Faith. "I feel so bad for you. It's got to be terrible not knowing all that stuff."

"It's hard, but hopefully, in time, they might return."

"Please don't get mad, but I kind of hope they don't."

Surprise rolled over Faith. "Why would you wish that?"

"Because if you ever remember, you might leave us. If you don't remember, you'll stay here."

Faith gulped a lungful of air. Sierra had a simplistic view

of events. She embraced her and brought her close. "Honey, I have no plans to leave any time soon. I enjoy being here with your daddy and Uncle Jack, and especially with you. You are very special. Okay?"

The little girl nodded, sniffing her tears away. Faith had tears too, welling in her eyes, and she blinked them away. This child was so dear, and her heart swelled with passion.

The rumble of the truck's engine reached them. "Daddy! Daddy's back!"

Sierra jumped off the porch to greet him as he parked. Faith stood and smoothed out her shirt. Colby climbed from the cab and Sierra flew over and attached herself to his leg. Butterflies took off in Faith's stomach. She tried to read the emotions on Colby's face, but he shifted to a happy smile as he swung his daughter into the air, then caught her as she giggled merrily.

He reached the steps, gave her a big, long hug, and set her down. "Go on and play inside now, Button. I need to talk with Faith. I love you so much."

"I love you too, Daddy."

Once the child took her book back inside, he turned to Faith. She swore she saw a tear in his eye and her heart stalled. She gripped the porch railing, suddenly trembling.

"How did it go?"

He shook his head. "Leah was brutal. She's always been shrewd and evil, but today was a whole new level."

That didn't sound good at all. "Did you tell the judge about us?"

His chortle was harsh. "Oh yeah. Leah had a field day with that. If she has her way, I'll be arrested for reckless endangerment of a minor and you'll be locked up somewhere too. She also suggested you were faking the amnesia."

Faith's hand flew to her chest. "She said all that?"

Colby's nod was grim, and scary."

"What a terrible woman." Faith recalled the last moments with sweet Sierra and prayed that woman never got her clutches into the child and drove the innocence away.

"Yes." He reached out and took her hand and guided her to the porch swing. Once they were settled, she leaned her head against his shoulder. She heard his steady heartbeat. His arm reached around her shoulder and his hand rested against her arm.

Faith lifted her head briefly, turning to face him. "What I don't understand is why they decided to come after her now? After all these years? She'd be sent to live with complete strangers. Don't they realize how distressing that would be to her?" And her father. And to her.

"I've had lots of theories pop into my head about their timing, but I honestly don't know either. And neither one of them would tell me the truth if I asked."

Quiet fell over them like a blanket. Faith concentrated on Colby's heartbeats. "So what happens now?"

"We wait. Hopefully, I was able to convince the judge after all. Optimistically, he saw through Leah's drama. If not, we'll repeat it again with lawyers and the whole formal affair."

"Is there anything I can do to help convince the judge? Write him a letter?"

Colby smiled and squeezed her shoulder. His hand was warm and strong.

"Thank you, Faith, but I don't see how that would sway

him. He has plenty of letters already. I just wish I knew why Leah and Darryl have popped up after all these years. What gives with them?"

"That sure would explain a lot. I'll do what I can to help. In the meantime, we have to have faith that the judge will see you are clearly the better parent."

Colby felt the giant sigh escaping him, turning frosty into the gathering twilight. He stared out at the five-foot star Jack found at the thrift store at The Plaza and mounted on the barn loft. It glowed a soft alabaster. "That sure would make a great Christmas gift if he did."

Colby went out to the barn to check on the horses. There wasn't any particular reason to, he was just restless. After dinner, he felt the urge to stay close to Sierra and Faith. They popped a big bowl of popcorn and settled in front of the television and watched The Grinch and Frosty. Afterward, he took Sierra to bed and read her a short story. Her eyelids grew heavier as he turned the pages. By the time he reached page twenty-one, she was out.

His heart twisted as he gave her cheek a soft kiss, dimmed the ballerina table light, and let himself out. It would kill him if he had to give her up. He'd rather sacrifice his arm before surrendering his child. Didn't anyone understand that?

Faith met him at the bottom of the stairs.

"Are you alright?" she asked, her voice honey smooth.

He cleared his throat, clearing away the tension and unshed tears. "Fine. I'm fine."

Her look, complete with narrowed eyes, raised brows,

and crooked grin proved she believed otherwise. Evidently, he would not be able to lie to her. She took his hand and led him back to the sofa by the sparkling tree. It was surreal to sit next to her, their thighs touching, warm through the denim, in a room that nearly spun around them with Christmas magic.

He leaned his head on her shoulder. "I'm just worried. The whole custody thing." He closed his eyes, and breathed in the tropical scent of her shampoo, still fresh hours after her shower.

She cuddled him close, softly patting his cheek. "I know. It's scary. I can only imagine how much this is hurting you. But try to have faith, Colby. Together, we will see this through. Together, all right?"

"Yeah." He didn't quite have her optimism, but he truly appreciated her efforts. And the enjoyable feeling of her soft body pressed next to his. He could be tempted to stay next to her all night, but by a supreme effort, he pulled himself away. He blinked back the tears in his eyes, kissed her hand, and brushed his thumb over the inside of her wrist. Such soft, silken skin!

"Sweetheart, I wish you could pour some of that optimism into a bottle so I could drink it. But since that's not possible, I'll just have to lean on you and your positiveness. But I think I'll go to bed now. Good night, Faith."

Now he followed the moonlight to the barn and wandered among the stalls, listening to horses' nicker and snort. A few poked their heads over the stall doors to see who was disturbing their sleep. He offered a friendly pat as a means of compensation.

"Sorry, guys. Just a lot on my mind." He murmured to the animals. He picked up a strand of hay from the floor and twirled it between his hands. He'd never felt so helpless.

The sound of boots on the wooden boards made him jump. A beam from a flashlight bobbed in his direction.

"Colby?"

"Yes. Jack?" He smiled as his friend flipped off his flashlight and sat on a bale of hay. His gaze was similar to what Faith's had been earlier. With a heavy sigh, he settled down on another bale, still twirling the strand of hay.

"So, how'd it go with your in-laws? I never had a chance to ask where little miss wasn't around or nearby."

"Ex in-laws." Colby bit the words out. He hated anything that connected him to them.

Jack nodded. "Uh, huh. Judging by the sour look on your face, it didn't go well. You look like you just bit into an overripe lemon."

He might prefer that to this custody hearing. "She accused me of reckless endangerment of Sierra. Of neglecting her basic needs. And just about everything else a man can do wrong."

Jack snorted. "Never did like that old bat."

"I used to. Now I'm trying real hard to remember why."

"It would have to be a short list of reasons." Jack chuckled. "How 'bout the old man?"

Colby sighed and shrugged. "He follows Leah's lead. He just pointed out how he and Leah were so much better equipped to meet Sierra's every need, while I was struggling to provide the basics." He frowned. "They like to be compared to the Rockefellers or Vanderbilts, but I know better. Leah'd never admit it, but I know she used to buy knock-off stuff off the clearance racks."

Jack tossed a fistful of straw down. "I never did care for their superior, snotty attitude."

"And I've never felt so dirty. To them, we are just a bunch of filthy men."

Jack yawned and stood up. "Colby, old pal, you gotta believe it will be alright. She ain't gotta like you. You ain't needing to like her. Now, I'm turning in. Night."

"Night, Jack." Colby's gaze followed Jack until he swung the barn door shut, blocking out the pale moonlight. His anger at Leah slowly subsided, replaced by gnawing worry she had convinced the judge. Something that could only be described as terror clawed through him.

Moonlight poured through Faith's window. Tired of tossing, she climbed out of bed and pulled the curtain over the pane. She could not get Colby's expression and soft comment out of her mind. His fear stabbed her heart. If he lost Sierra to those people, she might hate them for the rest of her life.

Now, as the clock read two-thirty, she yawned, but sleep would not come to her. Her thoughts tumbled in a jumbled mess like those pictures of tumbleweeds taking over roads and fields that Jack had shown her.

She had promised to stay, and talk of marriage excited her, and becoming Sierra's mom filled her with awe and joy. It all seemed so wonderful and perfect. But what if she were already married, and a mother?

In the pale light, she rubbed the circle on her finger. If she had children, they would be about Sierra's age, or perhaps younger. Someone had to be watching them all this time. Why hadn't that person reported her as missing?

It would be a good assumption she had been staying at the hotel in town. Crazy Woman only had one hotel, yet the proprietor had no missing guests. So where had she come from?

She felt like the only place she was wanted was here, at Tica, with the people she wanted to be with. So why couldn't she leave the possibilities of her past life behind?

What was out there that she needed to know? And what would knowing it do to Colby and Sierra?

CHAPTER **TWELVE**

"More coffee, Patsy?" Faith asked her guest.

"Goodness, no, but thank you. Your coffee has more grounds than a spring pond has tadpoles."

Faith drew back, stunned. Frog-loving Sierra had already shone her pictures of millions of swimming tadpoles. She peeked at the carafe. Perhaps. "Colby's never said anything," she said slowly.

Patsy reached across the table and patted Faith's arm. "Colby never would, sweetie."

Faith smiled. She had met Patsy and Hank Perkins at the dance. They owned the Wilde Acres Ranch. Turned out they were neighbors, in a how-the-crow-flies distance. She was learning time and locations were different here than she somehow expected them to be. She dusted off the apple-designed tablecloth. "No, I suppose he wouldn't."

Pasty stopped by for a neighborly chat, bringing her seven-year-old daughter, Trish. Now Sierra and Trish lounged in the living room, working on coloring books. Faith caught a glimpse of them, both laying on their bellies on the floor, stocking feet waving in the air as they giggled and traded crayons.

Another beautiful scene she would treasure.

"Now, before I forget, Colby had been asking around, inquiring about any newcomers to the area. He might want to know this if you could pass it on; my Hank spotted a couple city-slicker men driving a long, shiny car last Monday. Then he saw those same men walking over near the back of our spring pasture yesterday. Hank didn't engage them, because they weren't trespassing, but he said he felt funny knowing they were walking around out there."

Something sliced through Faith, a mix of heady excitement tinged with sorrow. Those men were part of her past. She just knew it, deep in her heart. And they were here! She had to learn more.

She plied Patsy with questions, making a map in her mind. With the coffee and pound cake gone, Patsy stood to leave. "You'll remember to tell Colby about those men?"

"Of course. I'll even make a note of it." After seeing her guest to the door and off with a wave, she dashed to the kitchen drawer. Taking paper and pen, she scribbled a note.

Colby, Patsy was here for a visit and said her husband noticed well-dressed men near their spring pasture. I know they are part of my past. Lately I feel so strongly that I want to remain in your life, and Sierra's, here at Tica. I want to be a permanent part of your life. But, Colby, please understand I have to go find these men and find out who I am. I can't be your Faith until I know, and these men can help me unlock that door. And, darling, once I know my past, I will come back to you to create a future. Faith

She wondered how she was going to leave while she still had to be here for Sierra. If she waited for Colby, he'd want to come along. As she considered her options, Jack strolled in. He barely made it to the coffee stuff, and she was on him.

"Jack! I have an errand to run. Can you stay with Sierra? Just for about an hour?"

"Sure, I reckon so."

"Thank you." She handed over the sealed note. "Can you give this to Colby? It's very important."

Going outside, she wryly eyed his battered pickup. "A child of seven drives it. With help. You can drive it, Faith." Bolstered, she climbed behind the wheel. The steering wheel was huge. Sucking in a breath, her heart beating, she turned the key. With a grunt, it roared to life. Gingerly, she shifted the gearstick on the floorboard. It screeched like Sierra's rooster. She jumped, then she stomped on the pedals and tried again. The truck inched forward. Exhaling, she tapped the gas.

Eventually she ran out of the road and then the path and finally reached the end of a trail. She stopped in what had been the parking area of the church. A weathered white building, barely discernable as a church except for the small cross atop the steeple, stood next to a towering oak tree. The equally faded sign read *Cornelius Church of Faith.*

Faith? She blinked at the name before she turned the truck off and eased out a grateful sigh. What an experience with the beast! Maybe she'd walk back after finding the men. They had to still be in the area. Her gut told her so. One thing having amnesia had taught her was to follow her gut feelings.

She stood, surrounded by woods and hills, and rotting remnants of the old Cornelius town which slowly opened to lush ranch land. She turned in a circle and knew this land was the reason she was out here. Something to do with this land. This area. This *what?*

She walked, driven by instinct, a guiding finger leading her through the trees, and up the hills. She was thankful for the sturdy boots Colby insisted she have. Her mouth felt dry as cotton, and she regretted not bringing a thermos of water.

Topping the hill, she headed down into the valley. Sunlight glinted off the river and…glass. She squinted. Hidden in the trees sat a black car. Not a rusty truck but a real car, clean and not coated in rust or untold layers of dirt. Her heart skipped a couple of beats.

Eagerly, she trotted down, and pushed the branches out of her way. She slowed down, listening for the sound of voices. Hoping to hear voices. *Needing* to hear them.

Finally, she heard them talking softly, long before she spotted them. Ducking low, she watched.

Two men, one tall and wide-shouldered, the other a few inches shorter and slender. Both looked to be about mid-thirty. Each sported neatly trimmed dark hair, one had a mustache and goatee. They both had her same olive skin complexion. Both wore slacks, loafers, dress shirts, and sport coats. Her pulse raced, knowing they were connected to her past. No names came to mind. Their conversation was too soft for her to catch more than a stray word. She had to get closer. Her gut warned caution, but she had to catch them before they left. They would know her.

A twig snapped under her boot, and she froze, her breath held. They turned and the wide-shouldered man slowly smiled at her. With caution still flashing in her mind, she took heart at his welcoming smile. He *did* know her.

"Isobel. You finally surfaced." He ran his eyes up and

down her, and then wrinkled his nose in obvious distaste. "I hardly recognized you in those bohemian rags."

Isobel. Isobel? Was that her?

She didn't know. She didn't know! His voice pulled at a memory, and she longed to yank it free of her mind. "You know me?"

Instead of answering, he took two steps toward her and instinctively she backed away, yielding to the screaming caution. His smile did not seem so welcoming now. Her hands went up in defense, and she marveled at her body's automatic reaction to him.

"You were a bad girl to run away from me, Isobel. You embarrassed me in front of my friends. You made me need to lie to cover up your misdeed. We had to return home for some business, and I had to lie for your sins. But now we're back and you are going to pay. Again." His voice dropped to a low growl and his eyes narrowed. "I would have thought you learned your lesson by now."

She inhaled and whirled. He was faster. He caught her shoulder and spun her around, slamming her into the nearest tree. Breathless, Faith stared up into his hard eyes, void of any compassion. She looked over at the other man, hoping for help, but he was busy smoking a cigarette and staring in the opposite direction. Why wasn't he helping her?

"Help me!" She tried waving to get his attention, but he remained deaf and oblivious to her cries.

"Shame, shame. You know he won't help you. His job is to protect us, not save you from a punishment."

She twisted, desperate to get away. This man held her in an iron grip as he smoothed back his hair with his free hand. His gold rings sparkled in the dappled sunlight. Finished, he turned his full attention back to Faith, his lips lifting into a snarl and eyes narrowing to slits. She knew they were not friends.

"Let me go, please. I don't know you. And you are hurting me!" She tried jerking away again, feeling like she was wrestling an octopus with legs of steel vices.

"Since you don't learn with repetition, maybe I need to break a leg or two so you can't run away. Would that do it, Isobel?"

She swallowed against the fear as her throat constricted. He would do it; she knew he would do it.

"No, please don't." She whispered in terror.

Faith felt him coil his arm like a snake and braced herself. He hurled her away from the tree and to the ground. She landed with a thud, forcing the air from her lungs. He grabbed her by the arms and lifted her as if she were a ragdoll and slammed her against the tree. He grabbed a handful of hair and pounded her head into the trunk. Her skull cracked, she felt sure her brains were leaking out and she dug her fingers into the bark to stay upright. Stars exploded behind her eyes.

She'd have dropped if he still hadn't been holding her. He gave her shirt collar a snapping jerk and hammered her against the tree again. She felt the warm blood flow down her face. She clutched the tree as her world spun.

Isobel. Now she remembered, memories tumbling loose through the pain and the swirling haze. Like startled butterflies lifting off, she mentally reached out to grab as many as she could. She was Isobel Cantillini. Her fiancé, Roberto, was giving her yet another pounding. And he most likely would break a leg or two before he was finished. His bodyguard and partner, Ricardo, was always present, and never any help to her. And they were to be married soon. Once they returned to Philly from this venture, of which Roberto was obsessed.

He learned there was natural gas in this area. He wanted to buy out the ranchers dirt cheap, rip out the farmsteads, and mine the natural gas. While on a scouting expedition, she finally saw a chance to escape Roberto. She'd slid off her engagement ring and ran until she could run no more. Until she collapsed and Colby found her.

Now he would haul her back to Philadelphia and make up something about how she was injured in some accident and force her to go through with the wedding before she could recover. As he berated her and assaulted her, no longer feeling the pain, she thought of Colby.

How she wished she had just stayed with him and become his Faith. It would have been so easy, if only she could have let her past go. Isobel had nothing to live for. As Faith, she had so much. Colby. Sierra. Even funny Jack. And now it was all lost. Foolish, foolish woman.

As darkness dropped down on her, she cried for Colby, for Sierra, and for the life they could have had. In the darkness of her mind, she heard the anguished wails of a woman in distress. The maiden. The legend was right. The Crazy Woman of the creek would never allow anyone to remain happily in love.

CHAPTER THIRTEEN

Colby returned home, still not sure if keeping the story of the ring from Faith was an honorable thing or a coward's way out. What was he afraid of?

"Losing her." He laughed at his own indecision as he parked the truck. He'd been running both scenarios through his mind since he left Crazy Woman and still didn't know. He absently noted the truck was gone and wondered why Jack would leave when he knew he was in town. Unless he took the truck out to check something in the pastures. He shrugged. Right now, he had more on his mind than where Jack could be running off to.

He entered the house. Jack and Sierra sat at the kitchen table, playing a card game. Go Fish. He looked around.

"Where's Faith?"

"She had to go check on something, but she left you that note by the coffee. Said it was important."

Faith took the truck? That surprised him. Until he read the note, his breath leaving him in a rush. He grabbed for the counter.

Jack looked up from the cards. "You okay, Colby?"

"I… I gotta go." He handed Faith's note to Jack, kissed Sierra, and walked outside. Cold fear shot through him. What if these people convinced her to go back to her old life? Would she really leave him? Could she?

Once he was back in the truck, he called Hank and Patsy. After a few minutes, he hung up, sure he had a good idea where they'd seen those people. And where he might find Faith. Last, he pulled his gun belt out from under the seat and checked the cylinder of his .45 Colt.

When he reached where Faith left his truck, he parked the Wagoneer next to it. According to Hank, they were seen between Bald Gap and the Crazy Woman Creek. He heaved a sigh. Back to the Crazy Woman range and that dismal valley of Cornelius. Well, he found her there once, and he'd find her there again.

Unless she already left with the men. Her fiancé.

Sour bile rose in his throat at the thought, the memory of that ring, and he quickened his pace. He topped Bald Gap and eyed the valley. He spotted the sunlight reflecting off some glass. A car perhaps. Hank said he'd seen a dark car. Then he spotted the people. And his blood went cold as he recognized the woman on the ground.

Faith!

Racing down the incline, lungs laboring for air, he took in the scene. The slender man stood idly by, disinterested. The beefy guy was at Faith's side. He must be her man. The one who bought her that repulsive ring. She appeared to be unconscious. Had she fallen?

Then the beefy guy reared back and lifted a foot, his intention clear. Red anger tore through Colby as he raced on. Gasping for breath, he barreled shoulder first into the man like two dueling grizzly bears. The force lifted both men off the ground. They landed, Colby on top, and he scrambled to grab the man.

The other fellow who had been standing idly by now sprang to life, reaching under his jacket. "Stay back!" Colby barked." Holster your weapon!"

The stranger beneath Colby grabbed Colby's gun, yanking it out of the holster. Desperation tore through Colby, and he wrestled for the weapon. He gripped the man's forearm and banged his wrist along the ground, hard enough for him to loosen his grip. Before he could snatch it up, the man knocked it out of the way. Now neither could reach it.

He slugged his fists into the man's chest. Enraged, he only saw Faith lying helpless and this scumbag trying to hurt her. He dared to kick her while she lay vulnerable! Blood roared in his ears and red colored his vision. He drove his fists repetitively, raining blow after blow upon the man and receiving equal slugs in return. He scarcely felt the impacts. Slowly, he turned the fight to his favor. He was going to pound this guy into the ground.

Suddenly he couldn't breathe. A vise gripped around his neck, hauling him off the man. Colby yanked at the arm holding him and struggled to inhale. The other man who accompanied this one now held him almost immobile. The scumbag who beat Faith moaned and writhed on the ground. Colby's vision clouded over, and his chest burned. The red rage he'd felt just moments ago slowly faded as his lungs cried desperately for air.

He would not last much longer. The man holding him was immovable as a tree. His arm, locked around his neck, was strong and muscular as a longhorn bull. Clearly, he defended the other man as a protective cow.

The corners of his sight grew black. His mouth opened in a vain attempt to suck in a breath. He grew dizzy. The only thing holding him up was the bull-strong grip behind him.

Through the smoky haze of his mind, he heard the cries of a woman in agony. Faith! Energy surged through him, but it wasn't enough to escape the strength of the man holding him. He painfully twisted his face to where Faith lay on the ground, still motionless. The sorrowful cries had not come from her. Could it be the maiden from the legend of the Crazy Woman Creek?

He pictured both Faith and Sierra, and how they were now lost to him. The dark haze covered him as his oxygen starved lungs surrendered and tears stung his eyes.

A gunshot rang out, echoing around them. The man holding Colby spooked like a yearling colt and Colby slid to the ground, gasping for air and clawing the grass for his gun. Hoofbeats thundered around him, and finally he located the Colt and gripped it, then rolled over to address the new threat.

Jack sat there, seated upon his horse, his rifle trained on the brute who had tried to choke the life out of him just moments ago. Meeting Colby's eye, Jack grinned.

"Looks like you needed a hand. What's going on?"

He rasped for breath. "Long story. Hold these two vermin here." He motioned to the first man who had at some point climbed to his feet and now stood, sullen, wobbling, as welts popped up on his face. Colby sprinted to Faith and sank to his knees at her side.

Blood poured from her old scalp wound and many new wounds. Gently, he cradled her to his chest and brushed her hair away. His heart splintered at the sight and for a moment, he wished he'd killed the pile of crap who did this to her.

"Faith. Can you hear me, Faith?"

She moaned and pried one eye open. He realized the other was swollen shut and already turning black. Fresh rage covered him. He bent and kissed her split and bleeding lips. "Oh, Faith. Oh, honey. I am so sorry, Faith."

"Isobel," she whispered. "That's my real name. Isobel Cantillini. And he's my fiancé, Roberto Russo."

"You remember?" He wasn't sure he was glad about that.

"I remember everything. He is a bad man. He is cruel, heartless, and soulless."

He took her hand in his. "He will never touch you again. Now you know your past. And you will always be Faith to me. So what do you want to do with your future?"

She gave him a small smile, wincing at the discomfort. "I want to be your Faith. Forever."

That was all he needed to hear. He helped her up and together they limped back to Jack and the other men. Jack calmly sat his horse, rifle resting in the crook of his arm as he kept it trained on the two men. Colby eased Faith against a tree for support and approached the first man—Roberto—and met him eye to eye. He lifted his lip in a snarl.

"She is mine, from now on. Whatever brought you to our town is through. You're done. Take that cur and go," he growled, pushing him away with a grunt of disgust. "Never come back." He lifted his Colt and aimed it in Roberto's face, hoping the guy would just try something. His whole body ached for the man to do something stupid.

Behind him, Jack racked the rifle, the sound ominous in the quiet. The men huffed and puffed, but obediently slinked to their car.

Colby turned to Jack. "Where's Sierra?"

"I called Mrs. Watkins to come watch her."

"Thanks, pal. I never thought I'd be so glad to see you."

Jack grinned, his gaze still trailing the cowards as they backed their car up from its hiding spot. "Sorry it took me so long to get here. Y'all didn't leave me anything to drive but a tractor, so I had to make do with ol' Rusty here." He patted the neck of his horse who stomped one front foot in response.

"How did you know to come?"

Jack chuckled. "Way everyone was lighting out for here, I figured I'd have to come and see what the draw is."

Colby snorted. "I'd be glad to never see this area again." He left Jack to ensure they didn't double back and hustled back to Faith's side. She had slid down the tree trunk, and now lay in a fetal position, trembling like a leaf in the wind and his heart cracked. Was she in shock?

"Faith?" He took her into his arms, his heart wincing at her wounds. "Let's get you back home and cleaned up. Is anything broken? Should I take you to the hospital instead? Can you walk to the truck, or shall I carry you?" He paused for a breath.

"Isobel. That's who I was."

He paused before his tongue tripped over itself again. The name fit her, but he liked Faith better. He licked his lips. "Do you prefer to be called Isobel?" He hoped not.

Tears filled her eyes as she gently shook her head. "I only want to be your Faith. And Sierra's mom. Let Isobel fade away."

He wanted to burst into song. He might have laughed joyfully if she were not shaking so badly. Instead, he kissed her forehead. "That sounds good to me."

Jack came up beside them. "Ma'am, gotta say I've seen you look a whole lot better. But those vermin are gone and won't be back."

"I hope not." She breathed a long sigh. "I never want to see them again."

"Colby, I can tie Rusty to the bumper of the truck and drive back, and you can take Faith in the Wagoneer. It's a mite smoother ride."

Colby was grateful for his friend's suggestions. Now that his rage was simmering down, he was at a total loss on what to do. Confronted with Faith's injuries and her confession to be his, he was feeling like a babbling baboon. Jack's cool, steady presence was a true godsend. He nodded at Jack.

Ever so carefully, he stood, bringing Faith up with him, cradling her close to his side. They hobbled toward the Jeep. Halfway there, he cracked a grin.

"Does this remind you of another time?"

She smiled slightly. "Yes. He was going to break my legs."

"What?" Surely, he heard wrong.

"To keep me from running again. With two broken legs, I'd be at his mercy. If you had been even a few minutes later, we wouldn't be able to limp back."

Fresh rage spiked through Colby. Why hadn't he pulled the trigger when he had the chance? He glanced over at Jack, leading the horse about five paces behind them, and met his grim, tight-lipped expression and suspected Jack was asking himself the same question.

"He will never be able to hurt you again, Faith," he assured her, squeezing her hand. "Never. If he shows up at Tica, he'll be shot on sight like the mangy cur he is."

Jack caught up to them and patted Colby on the shoulder. "And I'll spread the word to the boys, with shoot on sight instructions, and we can all carry our weapons for a few days, just in case he gets any stupid ideas."

"You two have no idea how safe you make me feel. I can't believe my life under Roberto's control is finally over."

By the time they reached the vehicles, Faith's trembling had largely subsided. Colby nestled her on the front seat next to him and they began the slow drive back to Tica. Jack brought up the rear, moving slow enough for the horse, tethered to the truck's bumper, to keep up.

They reached the driveway and parked. Sierra was on the porch with Mrs. Watkins. She came running out.

"You're back!" she exclaimed. "I thought you would never get back." She stopped, staring at Faith, her eyes widening. "Faith! What happened to you?"

Colby looked from Faith to Sierra. How much should he explain to his daughter? "Well, Button, um…"

"Sweetie, I just had a small accident out in the woods. I'll be fine in a day or two."

Colby almost laughed at Sierra's doubtful expression. And Mrs. Watkins' equally surprised face.

The older woman reached for Sierra's hand. "Honey, why don't we go down to the Plaza and look for some flowers or candy for Faith? She looks like she'd appreciate that."

Faith silently mouthed the words "Thank you" to Mrs.

Watkins. "Yes, I would like that very much," she said to Sierra.

Colby handed over the keys to the Wagoneer to his neighbor. "Here, take my truck. There's about twenty bucks or so in the console." She nodded as she fisted the keys. "Come, sweetheart."

"I think that girl will have nightmares now," Faith said once they were out the driveway. "Do I look that bad?"

He studied her. She had one black eye, the other one swollen shut. Her lip was cut and bloodied, as was her left cheek. Her blouse and hair were full of dried leaves and bloody smears. Red marks of fingerprints marred her right forearm. He could only imagine what other marks and bruises she had under her clothes. His heart thumped in his chest, both for admiration of her strength and the pain she must be feeling. He rubbed his thumbs tenderly along her jawbone and stared deep into her eyes. "You look beautiful to me."

CHAPTER **FOURTEEN**

Two hours later, Faith enjoyed a soak in her bathtub and washed away what could be scrubbed. She sat huddled in the tub, crying, for so long her skin wrinkled like raisins by the time she emerged red-eyed and fresh-scrubbed. Sierra surprised her with a lovely bouquet of red roses, white carnations, lily of the valley, baby's breath, and more. The sweet, slightly tropical scent was indulgent. She had also purchased a small box of chocolates. Faith shared them with Sierra and Mrs. Watkins and Jack. Colby politely refused. But she knew his sweet tooth favored gummies and jellybeans, not chocolates.

Jack prepared a meal of cheeseburger soup and a green salad. Sierra plied Faith with questions about her 'accident in the woods'. After dinner, Jack disappeared, and Colby put Sierra to bed. After he finished reading her a story, he returned to where Faith sat in the living room, staring into the fire with a quilted blanket draped over her.

"Thought I'd find you here." He sat down beside her on the sofa. "Did you enjoy your bath?"

"Umm hmm. It was a fantastic tonic to the bruises and aches." So was the long cry.

"You smell like lavender."

"Scented Epsom salts."

They lapsed into silence. Colby's arm curled around her shoulder and his other hand softly gripped her hand. He must have cleaned up too, as he smelled like spice and musk.

The warm lighting from the Christmas tree washed over the room, filling it with a soft, white glow. Candles flickered, the fireplace popped, and the scents of burning wood and evergreen tree permeated the air. Cinnamon, citrus, and berries spiked the room with their fragrances. The quiet and stillness was welcoming and wholly inviting.

"I do like this room."

He snuggled her neck. "You and Sierra did a fantastic job decorating. I've never seen it look better. This will be the best Christmas Tica has ever seen."

She smiled and nestled up against his chest. His steady heartbeat felt comforting against her ear. "It already is." Christmas was two days away and he'd already given her the best present ever: freedom from her past.

And she had to tell him who she was. She cleared her throat, mentally preparing herself. "Colby…"

"How much do you remember?"

"Everything." Every horrible detail. "I want to share it with you."

His breath hitched. "Are you sure? You don't have to."

Faith was confident he wanted to know everything. She needed to get it all off her chest. She nodded in response to his question. "I want to. I need to." She swallowed, formulating her thoughts. Finally, she pulled away from Colby, brought the blanket tighter around her shoulders and faced him square.

"I... Isobel is...she was a mafia princess." She felt the ripple of shock roll over him.

"Mumm. Truthfully, that's not what I was expecting."

That surprised her. "What were you thinking?"

"I didn't really know." He shook his head. "But a mafia princess didn't show on my radar." He hugged her tight and traced her cheekbones. "So, tell me about... her. Isobel."

She thought for a moment, enjoying his gentle touch gliding over her face. "Not so different from many females born into the family. Brought up to be an ornament on a man's arm. Taught to keep her eyes open and mouth shut. My father ran a large mob—or family—in Philadelphia. He was the boss, or the king. My mother died when I was twelve. I was their only child."

"I would think that made you indulged and pampered."

She nodded. "It did, for a little while. Until I reached my latter teens. Roberto was my father's underboss, his second-in-command by then. I knew he was interested in me, and he was angered when I did not return his favor. Then my father died last year, under what many considered dubious circumstances. Roberto moved up to boss, and assumed I now belonged to him, as well as everything that was my father's. Our house, cars, money, and me. I was transferred over like livestock, or the rest of my father's assets.

"I found out after the funeral my father willed me to Roberto, with the intention to marry him. Roberto had some documents with my father's signature. I could not believe my father would simply will me away to a man I despised without even warning me.

"Roberto made our engagement public and never even

once asked my wishes. He took what he wanted by force, if necessary. He would not be told no." She shivered. "So when I resisted, he became…"

"That's okay, Faith. I get the rest of the picture." Colby traced her fingers and the palm of her hand with gentle strokes. "You don't have to explain any more. I wish I'd shot both those skunks when I had the chance. We could have dumped their bodies in the Crazy Woman Gorge where dead cows are dumped. No one would have noticed or cared about two more stinking carcasses of bull."

Faith managed a smile. "That's very noble of you, and a glorious image, but it's probably better you did not yield to your wishes. Now he has to go back to Philly and eat lots of crow. His consigliere and caporegimes might move to replace him and Ricardo with a new boss and underboss."

"That would be only fitting I think."

"Or he will bring his people back down here en masse. They would go through this town like a wildfire." She paused, terror striking her. "I can't imagine what they would do to Tica—or us." She gripped his shirt. "Colby, by sending them away beaten, and without me, you might have created a big problem."

He took her hands into his and kissed her knuckles. "Faith, my love, there was no way I was sending you back with those yahoos. None." He shook his head. "No. I couldn't. But if you decided not to be with me anymore, I'd buy you a ticket to the destination of your choice and get you on a train or bus and see you safely on your way. And then go sweep up my broken heart."

She smiled and placed her palm over his beating heart.

"I am very happy to stay here with you and Sierra, Colby

my love. But we should be prepared in case Roberto returns with his men."

"Not to worry." He wrapped his hand over hers, warmth spreading from his palm and sandwiching it between his chest and hand. "I'll spread the word. Every adult around here, and child over twelve, can pack a weapon for self-defense against evil critters. Sometimes they walk on two legs. If them yahoos try coming back here, they'll be spotted before they reach Henderson County and will find out what Texans can really do." He winked. "It ain't pretty."

His gaze dropped down to her left hand, and he gently traced the pale circle. "I haven't had time to tell you, but your ring has been found."

"How? By whom?" Not that she ever wanted to see the ugly gold and diamond engagement ring again. "You don't have it, do you?"

"No, but a rancher just over the Crazy Woman Creek found it on his land, not too far from where we first met. It's a big ol' rock, isn't it?"

"I hate it." she shivered.

He nodded. "Yep, I can see how. Don't blame you for ditching it. Anyway, Stan brought his treasure to Dimples, bragging how rich he was now. A few guys suggested he turn it over to the police, but he was firmly set on keeping it long enough to sell it for top dollar."

"It is worth several thousand dollars. Did you tell him you knew it was mine?"

Colby looked shocked. "Why would I do that? He might be persuaded to hand it over. What would I do with that ugly ol' thing?"

She lifted her shoulder. "Whatever you wanted to do with it."

He nuzzled along her neck, raising the hairs along her neck. "I never want to see it again. If I decide to offer you a ring in exchange for some vows, I plan on buying you a much nicer ring. It won't have all the size and bling that one did, but it will be bought and given in love."

She smiled. And bravely moved the blanket to invite him to join her. "When do you think you would want to make such an offer?"

"Not sure yet, but let's say next year is looking bright indeed."

"These decorations look so pretty, so why do we have to take them down?" Sierra complained to Faith.

Faith smiled at the petulant child. "Because Christmas is over, the old year is gone, and it's time to embrace January and the new year to come. Part of that means packing away our Christmas decorations until the next holiday rolls around. Then we can decorate even better than ever."

Sierra looked doubtful and Faith chuckled. "Come here, sweetie, and give me a hug." She knelt and opened her arms.

"I'm so glad you got your memories back. That was the best Christmas present ever."

Sierra was right. While she and Colby had not shared everything with the girl, they shared enough to make her holiday happy. Faith was shocked at how much joy Sierra got from knowing she knew her past, most importantly she felt comfortable staying on at Tica Ranch.

"Now Daddy has to marry you and you gotta say yes you will."

She hugged Sierra again, tears burning her eyes. "We've talked about maybe in the spring. We have a few things to work out first. And there's all sorts of planning to be done."

Not much planning, really, as she had no family to invite. They would just hold a simple affair for the locals and ranch crew. Colby suggested they trail ride out into the wilderness and camp for their honeymoon. Faith still wasn't sure how to decide on that.

Sierra gasped. "I know! I'll pick you a bouquet of wildflowers. There're some pretty ones that grow in the meadow. Some are blue, others are white, and a bunch are yellow! You can carry it and I can be your flower girl. We can wear flower wreaths in our hair. Matching ones, of course."

"Of course. I can't think of anything better." Faith laughed. "Now I need a dress. And your daddy needs a suit."

As they packed away the Christmas decorations, Sierra worked out most of the details for the wedding. Faith was surprised how much interest the girl had. Maybe she could grow up to be a wedding planner. That was a big business in Philly. The city of Brotherly Love had lots of weddings.

"Well, all done! We can just leave these boxes for the men to put up in the attic. Our part is finished." Faith reached out her hand to high five Sierra. As they slapped palms, she was drawn to the girl's smile. Suddenly, she wanted to be involved in each step of her life. As she grew, developed stronger relationships with friends, discovered boys, dated, drove legally, and had her many firsts. First dance, first serious boyfriend, first job, first day at college. Sometimes the firsts someone experienced were just as bittersweet and beautiful as the lasts.

"Can I go play now?"

"Sure, sweetie. Stay near the house, though. No riding off on Topper."

Once Sierra was gone, Faith withdrew a file of paperwork from the buffet drawer and sat down at the kitchen table with a pen. To remain Faith, and let Isobel disappear, she needed new documentation. They had checked with Colby's lawyer about how to do that, and he produced a folder of paperwork. Once completed, Faith needed to file it with the court, and they did their various processes with it. Within a few weeks, she would legally become Faith Avery Cantillini. And then, when the time was right and the flowers were in bloom, she would become Faith Avery Lonigan. *Avery*. Another lovely name Colby came up with. He said he simply liked the name and knew of no one in particular with it. She liked it as well and decided to adopt it as her new middle name, letting Marie fade away too. She smiled as she set pen to paper, filling in the blanks and boxes.

Faith turned the burner down to simmer and covered the stew pot. She inhaled the spicy aroma of bubbling chili. Warmth radiated from the burner. Yeasty butter rolls waited in the oven and fresh coffee percolated on the counter. She smiled in satisfaction. She was getting this ranch life down. Now that she knew what her past life was like, and how much she had hated it, she was even more inclined to learn how to live like a Texas rancher. This morning she even braved Buster's aggression to collect the chicken eggs.

Movement outside the window caught her attention. Colby and Jack rode back into the yard. Colby removed his hat and removed the dust by slapping it against his thigh. Her heart hammered at the sight of Colby astride Ben, sitting straight and tall, his silhouette proud and rugged.

She gave them time to put their horses in the stalls and then took the envelope that arrived earlier and stepped out onto the porch. The sun slowly sank behind the horizon, painting the sky in early shades of red and orange. Another beautiful sunset was on tap. Maybe after dinner, she and Colby could settle on the porch swing and watch.

She bypassed Sierra, who was playing with her dolls at the base of the big tree next to the house. She gave the girl a smile and gentle squeeze on her shoulder before heading to the barn.

"I'll be right back, sweetie. Dinner is almost done."

She clutched the envelope, drew in a breath, and entered the dim lighting. She heard Colby and Jack laughing and the snort of a horse, then the stomp of hooves on wood. Jack murmured a soothing word to his horse. She followed the sounds. This was Colby's world. Hay, straw, smells of horses, leather, sweat, and dirt. Sounds of saddles creaking, horses blowing, water sloshing, grain spilling into buckets, and boots on wooden floors.

She discovered she liked this world more each day. So different from her old life. She never wanted to return to big city life. Here, her soul felt at peace and her heart light.

"Hey, honey, how long have you been standing there?"

Colby's voice jerked her from her thoughts. He was smiling at her, warm and tender, awakening little shivers of excitement within her. He stood beside his horse, brush in hand.

"Just a moment." She glanced at Jack, also busy brushing his horse. "Dinner will be ready in just a few minutes. And this came earlier, special delivery with signature required. I hope you don't mind me signing for it."

"No, of course not." Colby set the brush aside, gave Ben a gentle pat, and reached for the envelope. His smile faded as he read the return address. "It's from the courthouse. Wanna bet it's the judge's decision?"

"So soon?"

Colby nodded. "He said he wouldn't need much time to decide on the next course of action." He gripped the envelope.

"I got Ben. You two go see what that judge has to say." Jack offered. He unclipped his horse and led it away.

Colby took Faith's hand and led her to a bale of hay. "Have a seat, and we'll read it together."

As Faith settled next to him on the prickly seat, he broke the seal and slid a finger to rip the top. He pulled the single page out, shook it open and wrapped his arm around Faith's shoulder. She nestled against his chest, so she could also read the page.

Within seconds, she pulled away, noticing his tight lips and sag to his shoulders. "Colby, I am so sorry. I was hoping he would…" Words failed her, and a sob rose up. She hiccupped it out.

"Now, now, honey. It's not the end. It just says he needs more information and time to make the right decision. We can mount a new defense and make sure he does make the best decision."

He set the letter aside, took her hand in his, and cupped her chin with his other hand. Gently, he dropped his lips to hers. She met his kiss and melted into the warmth. His beard grazed her chin and she smiled, liking the scruffy texture. Somewhere in the distance, she heard the clip clop of horse hooves echoing on the wooden floorboards. The steady beat echoed the pat, pat, pat, of her own heartbeat as Colby held her and kissed her almost senseless. She'd never known a man who could kiss her so thoroughly and so gently and with so much passion and desire as Colby.

"Well? What's the judge say?"

Jack stood before them, amusement in his eyes but a serious draw to his mouth. He hooked his thumbs in his belt loops and cocked a hip.

Colby sighed. "He wants to meet and discuss this a bit more. We can hold off on the lawyers for right now and give it one more shot at a civil discussion."

Faith cleared her throat. "Colby, I'd like to attend with you. Perhaps I can help the judge make the right choice. If nothing else, we could be a unified front against your ex-mother-in-law's verbal barbs."

CHAPTER **FIFTEEN**

Faith walked beside Colby down the brightly lit corridor. His hand was linked with hers. His grip was firm but tender. She truly felt like they presented the unified front to battle for the right to keep Sierra. Their boots echoed a steady tattoo on the waxed, tiled floor.

"We check in here." He nodded to the door, with a frosted window. He held it open and gave her a smile as she passed by.

She waited as he checked them in, and they were ushered to a small waiting room. They were the only ones there—so far. They only waited a few minutes before Lucy's parents arrived. Already seated, Faith took a moment to size them up. As a mafia princess, she was trained to form accurate opinions on people within seconds. And instantly she knew these people did not really want Sierra to have their granddaughter. There was no genuine love and concern evident. So why the ordeal?

Colby gave a curt nod and crossed his arms. Faith had a better plan. As they were instructed to enter the chambers, she boldly approached Leah and extended her hand. "Hello, I am Faith Cantillini, Colby's fiancée. It's nice to meet you."

If she could have shocked the room more, she didn't know how. Colby's jaw swung open, and his eyes widened. Clearly, he never expected her to be civil to the enemy. However, she'd learned one can throw their opponent off balance by being the first to set the tone, especially if the adversary is expecting one reaction and getting caught off-balance by another. It was an old way to gain the advantage she'd acquired from her father.

Leah recoiled as if she'd spotted a serpent. "How do you do?" she finally said once she regained her wits. "I'm Sierra's grandmother. I see you've recalled your memories."

Oh, this old battle axe was a shrewd one. And not one to be underestimated. Faith grinned. "Yes, it was such a relief to have them finally knock loose." She exhaled dramatically. "I cannot tell you how unpleasant it is to not remember the details of one's life. However, since that period is over, Colby and I are now cleared to proceed with our marriage plans." She cast a look at Colby, who stood as though he'd just swallowed a mouthful of tadpoles. She cast him an affectionate smile. She excused herself from Leah and moved with Colby to their seats.

"What are you doing?" he whispered as they sat down.

"Trust me. I can read people. She's not in this for Sierra's benefit."

"That doesn't make me feel any better, Faith."

Before she could comment, the judge arrived. Introductions were made and the proceedings began. There was a general recap from the previous visit before the judge asked for new information. Colby offered they now were moving forward with the marriage plans since she'd regained her memories.

Back and forth they talked, with Leah trying to get any barb in she could. After a while, a court clerk entered the room and whispered near the judge's ear.

"I will now call for a short recess while I attend an urgent matter that just came up."

Once the judge left, an uneasy silence followed. After a moment, Leah excused herself.

"Be right back," Faith whispered to Colby. She followed Leah past the waiting room and watched as she sat on a bench in the hall. Leah exhaled deeply. Faith casually walked into view and approached the bench. Leah's eyes widened in surprise. Faith thought she looked uncomfortable at her appearance. She sat and leaned down with her elbows on her knees.

"You are not what I was expecting." Leah's sharp comment drew Faith up, she glanced over to her. "You're different."

"I'm not from Texas." Faith offered by way of explanation.

It was Leah's turn to study her. She tilted her head and squinted one eye. "Are you a mother? Have you had children? A daughter?"

"No."

"And you plan to use my granddaughter as your guinea pig?"

Faith ignored the harsh accusation in Leah's tone. She shook her head, meeting the older woman's steely eye. "Sierra is not a guinea pig. She is already well loved, and I only want to share her father's life and become a solid presence in her life as well."

Leah's eye roll said a lot. As a mafia princess, Faith had been schooled to never compromise with anyone outside the family. Never share personal information. As Faith, soon to be a rancher's wife and mother to Sierra, she felt a new desire. She turned her body to fully face Leah, offering honesty, and took a breath.

"I am a daughter, though. My mother died when I was young, and I was raised by my father. He did what he felt was the best he could do. I had everything money could offer. However, I did not have his love. At least not openly showed, so I never had to question it or ask for it." She paused. "I can assure you that was hard on me. I needed my father, and he wasn't available even though he was physically nearby. Therefore, I can see how much Colby openly loves his daughter. Sierra never has to question it because it is always there on display. She makes him proud, makes him laugh, makes him cry, and every emotion you can think of, because his every thought is for that little girl."

Again, she paused, seeing chips of Leah's armor fall aside. "To lose Sierra would be the worse loss possible for Colby. And for me."

Leah swallowed convulsively. She looked away, and then back to Faith. "I lost my daughter." Her fingers worked the loose fringe of her scarf. "Lucy left, never told us. Her things are gone. She won't answer her phone." Her eyes misted over. "She left us, her father and I."

Just as she left Colby and Sierra. Faith reached out to pat Leah's arm. "I am sorry. That must feel terrible. Uncertain. When did this happen?"

Leah's fingers worked the fringe more, almost frantically. "Four months ago. I don't think she's coming back."

Faith put the last pieces together. The question of why

Lucy's parents wanted Sierra was no longer a mystery. She exhaled and took Leah's hand into hers. The older woman blinked and wiped her eyes.

"You must think I'm a foolish old woman."

Faith shook her head. "No, I think your daughter made a foolish mistake. I am asking you to please not make another mistake out of pain and desperation."

"What else can we do? We're here now, and the judge is waiting."

She grinned. "I have an idea. If you're willing."

CHAPTER SIXTEEN

Colby prided himself as being a calm, patient man, but when Faith walked out after Leah, his blood pressure spiked. His anxiety almost had him climbing the walls. It was all he could do to stay in his seat and stare mystified at Daryl. The judge returned and glanced around.

"What happened to the ladies?"

"They had to step outside for a moment, Sir."

The older man huffed, stared at the time, and shuffled files around. Colby was sure he was going to have a stroke if they didn't return soon.

The door swung open, and his heart constricted. He watched Leah come in, take her seat, and politely fold her hands on the table as if she were praying. She appeared different, but Colby couldn't put a finger on what changed. Faith came in next. She sent him a small grin and a long wink as she took her seat next to him.

Her actions did nothing for his anxiety. What the hell was going on?

"Is everyone ready to resume?"

Leah spoke first, "Your Honor, Ms. Cantillini and I have reached an agreement that we'd like to share."

Colby gripped the table's edge, his mind swirling. Leah reached an agreement with Faith? *What the hell?*

"Faith?" he whispered as low as he could muster. She reached for his hand.

"Proceed." The judge motioned with a wave of his hand.

Leah began. "My husband and I wish to stop this suit, contingent on the following terms: Sierra is to remain with her father and Ms. Cantillini. In an effort to get to know our granddaughter, we will travel to Crazy Woman once a year, at Christmastime, and visit for up to one week. Sierra can travel to Dallas over the summer school break and visit with us."

Colby listened; sure he was misunderstanding. He looked over at Faith. She contributed to the terms as well. It felt like a dream when the judge asked if all parties were in favor of the agreement. He muttered in the affirmative, not sure what was going on.

"If all parties agree, so it shall be. The clerk shall draw it up and I will have signed copies mailed to both addresses by the end of the week. Thank you for your cooperation."

EPILOGUE

"I don't know how you accomplished all this, Faith, but this has been the very best Christmas I have ever known."

Faith leaned back on the sofa and closed her eyes. Colby worked his thumbs into her feet. The lotion smelled like gardenia and filled the room with its sweetness. The citrus blended tea at her elbow wafted into the air. The mesquite from the fireplace sparked and sizzled. She could die happy right now.

"I didn't know you were so good at massages, but please don't stop."

Colby slashed her a wicked grin. "I don't intend to. With Sierra at the movies with her grandparents, we have two hours all to ourselves. I'm thinking after we finish this massage, and our tea, a shared bath might be in order." He moved up from her arches to her ankles. "You pulled off a miracle."

"Umm, a Christmas miracle. I miss the tree and all those pretty decorations."

"Maybe Jack and I will have to haul them all out of the attic tomorrow."

She shook her head. "No, don't bother. I had an idea. How do you feel about Sierra going to her grandparents after our wedding, and we can go on a real honeymoon? Maybe we can go somewhere exotic or picturesque."

Colby moved up her calf, working the muscles, then her thighs. "We can go anywhere you want. I just want my ring on your finger. Tomorrow, we go ring shopping."

"Christmas in Crazy Woman and being here at Tica has been so unbelievably wonderful. You and Sierra, and even Jack, have made me so happy." She shivered as Colby passed her thighs and moved up, grazing her flat abdomen, pausing to cup her breasts, trace her collarbone, and finally come to rest on either side of her jaw. He gazed deep in her eyes, until she was sure she'd be lost in the depths.

"Sweetheart, you have made this the best Christmas season I have ever had. You made my little girl so happy. You brought life and joy to all of us here at Tica. You guaranteed my daughter will stay here with us." His voice cracked with emotion. "I cannot wait to make you fully mine as a wife and a life partner. Faith, I love you so very much."

Before she could think to respond, he claimed her lips in a kiss, deep and long as the state of Texas.

Eager to hear what's next for Ryan Jo Summers?

Join her mailing list!

www.ryanjosummers.com/contact.html

Don't miss out on your next favorite book!
Join the Satin Romance mailing list
www.satinromance.com/mail.html

THANK YOU FOR READING

Did you enjoy this book?

We invite you to leave a review at your favorite book site, such as Goodreads, Amazon, Barnes & Noble, etc.

DID YOU KNOW THAT LEAVING A REVIEW...

- Helps other readers find books they may enjoy.
- Gives you a chance to let your voice be heard.
- Gives authors recognition for their hard work.
- Doesn't have to be long. A sentence or two about why you liked the book will do.

ABOUT THE AUTHOR

Ryan Jo Summers writes from the beautiful Blue Ridge Mountains, usually with a couple of dogs at her feet and at least one cat spread out over her desk. She is a sucker for homeless and traumatized fur-babies.

Her writing has appeared in trade journals and regional and national magazines. She has numerous novels, novellas, and anthology contributions all published in the romance genre and assorted subgenres. Some have placed well in national writing contests.

Aside from writing, Ryan Jo likes to work in her garden, gather with family and friends, and cook. paint, and read. She enjoys a good game of chess, or a challenging word find puzzle and watching fish swim in an aquarium.

Website: www.ryanjosummers.com
Blog: summersrye.wordpress.com
Facebook: www.facebook.com/RyanJoSummersAuthor

ALSO BY RYAN JO SUMMERS

WITH SATIN ROMANCE

Novels/Novellas

Glimpse Eternity

It Happened at the Park

Wild Whispers

Holiday Romance

Magic in the Snow

Christmas at Crazy Woman Creek

Anthologies

Coffeecake Chaos in Food & Romance Go Together Vol. 1

www.ingramcontent.com/pod-product-compliance
Lightning Source LLC
LaVergne TN
LVHW090610110826
845146LV00001B/330